LONG FALL
FROM
HEAVEN

LONG FALL
FROM
HEAVEN

A NOVEL BY GEORGE WIER
AND MILTON T. BURTON

CINCO PUNTOS PRESS EL PASO, TEXAS

Printed in the United States.

First Edition: 10 9 8 7 6 5 4 3 2 1

Library of Congress Cataloging-in-Publication Data

Wier, George.
  Long fall from heaven / by George Wier and Milton T. Burton. —First edition.
    pages cm
  ISBN 978-1-935955-52-8 (pbk. : alk. paper);   E-book ISBN 978-1-935955-53-5
  1. Ex-police officers—Fiction. 2. Serial murder investigation—Texas—Fiction. 3.
Galveston (Tex.)—Fiction. 4. Mystery fiction. I. Burton, Milton T. II. Title.

PS3623.I3846L66 2013
813'.6—dc23

2013010653

• • •

Book and cover design by Blue Panda Design Studio

• Arlington, Virginia
AUGUST 1943

[1]

He paced the long floor in the night. Twenty-eight steps the long way, nine steps the width of the old hardwood floor. After the first hour of the first night he knew the square footage down to the inch. From there it was a quick extrapolation to determine the cubic area, given the fourteen-foot antebellum ceilings. He loved the old house, the way the floors creaked and groaned. He also hated it. The scent of old resin and yellowing linen wallpaper hung in the air, the constant reminder of age and a dissolution held in long abeyance. The house should have been shelled or burned during the Civil War, but somehow the old building had escaped that insane bloodbath. It was likely one of only a few.

At night, he could see the dim glow of the Capitol above the trees that hemmed in the old mansion, but only when the lights were out inside. He could navigate fine indoors using only moonlight. But even when there was no moon, his perceptions were sharp—you didn't have to see a thing to know it was there. You had to be able to *feel* the night. And the night was his only friend.

The night was also quiet, but for the occasional outburst from one of his roommates. When one of them was pushed or fell 'beyond the beyond,' as he called it, they would cry or scream or gibber unintelligibly. This night they were quiet.

The military men needed him. They needed him against Hitler and Mussolini and Hirohito. He had little use for them. But there were steel bars on the windows and there was nowhere else to go.

One of the orderlies had taken to calling him 'Longnight.' He'd never had a nickname before. Somehow it fit him. Yes, the nights were long. Yes, he slept only during the day. He would *be* Longnight then, he decided.

Sometimes during the day, when they roused him and put him at a table with a writing tablet, Longnight would mock them by drawing cartoon figures instead of the ciphers. He sensed they wanted to hurt him, as if doing so would somehow make him do what they wanted. He knew there was no power on earth that could compel him.

He sensed the dawn long before it arrived. The orderly had come to check on him an hour before and left without saying a word. Maybe the man would go catch a catnap in the living room of the old house. Who knew? He sensed the dawn and stopped, staring out into the inky blackness beneath the line of trees across the lawn. There was something there. Something in the dark. But really, there wasn't—it was something in the darkness of his own mind, this he knew. It lived in the hollow places between thoughts. And it had a name.

Longnight realized he had stopped pacing. He stood, rapt. He exhaled, staring at the window four feet away with its heavy black steel bars. And waited.

It took a while, waiting there like that, unmoving, but finally the night breathed back at him. A low mist had arisen. Longnight watched it separate from the ground and begin to rise.

Longnight smiled. He stepped to the window and reached a hand between the ugly vertical bars. He breathed onto the window and wrote one of the equations the military men were looking for—the secret behind stabilizing Uranium 238.

He stepped back, waited for the figure to fade into nothingness and then wrote another figure, one with more far-reaching implications than simple nuclear fission—the secret for getting mankind to the stars:

$$\sum_{G=\emptyset}^{f \to \infty} = 2 \times 10^{-24}$$

That was the real secret after all. Nothingness. It was the one thing that the limited minds of most scientific men could not fathom. All along they were looking for some grand unifiying theory, and the answer was simply... nothing. And nothing was the answer they would never see. The answer was even contained within his new name, the nothingness of the long night.

Longnight watched as this figure also faded into the night.

At that moment he began planning his escape. After all, there was time. The World War was still on and it was stopping for no man. He could dole out hints at the true nature of the secret in return for day after day of breathing and still they would know less than nothing. And if he were to be deliberate, slow, he would find a way out. And then...

His name was Longnight, and the night was his only friend.

• Galveston, Texas

OCTOBER 1987

[2]

Micah Lanscomb's home was a repossessed Airstream parked in the alleyway behind Cueball Boland's pool hall. Its former silvery glory had dulled to a light orange, tarnished by the salt air from the Gulf, its buckled seams patched with various kinds of rubber cement—reds, blacks, translucents and grays. It looked like the tail section of a cooked lobster.

Micah's boss, Cueball Boland, owner of NiteWise Security Company, banged on the wall outside the door. It was still dark out. The sodium arc light made an eerie shadow of his aging and solid frame. The sky above was mostly overcast but an occasional dim star shined through. Not that Cueball spent much time looking at stars.

"What?" The voice from inside was muffled and sleepy.

"Need to talk to you," Cueball said.

No reply came. Instead the trailer creaked on its foundation of concrete pilings. Micah was getting himself up. Some day, Cueball thought, he would have to scrap the trailer and find proper quarters for his employee.

The door opened and Micah stood there in his underwear looking down at Cueball, his abdominal muscles rippling with his breathing. Micah shielded his eyes against the glare of the parking lot light. "Come in," he said. "Give me a sec to get some clothes on."

"Might as well put your security uniform on," Cueball said.

Cueball entered and stood in the cave-like darkness of Micah's living room. Micah shuffled off down the hallway and flicked on the light.

The room was neat as a pin—the way Micah kept everything with which he came in contact, be it possessions or relationships. From the bedroom, Cueball heard the sounds of hurried dressing and mild oaths.

"What gives?" Micah asked from down the hallway and a half-closed door.

"There's been a killing," Cueball said.

"Who?" Micah asked.

"Jack Pense."

"Damn," Micah responded. His bedroom door slapped the wall of the trailer and Micah's long stride brought him into view.

"Rusty called and woke Myrna up a few minutes ago. Somebody broke into the DeMour warehouse. They knocked Jack on the head, tied him up, and then—just for good measure—beat him to death."

"Shit," Micah said. "Anybody told Jenny?"

"No," Cueball said. "I'm sorry, Micah."

"Yeah. Me, too. Anything stolen over there?"

"Don't know. It's a big warehouse. I told Rusty to hold off calling the cops until we've arrived."

"Fine," Micah said and moved toward the door, but Cueball slowed his advance with a gently raised hand.

"Now, I know your first instinct is to go and tell Jenny. But she doesn't know yet and the news can keep for another few hours. Meantime, we've got work to do. Rusty is waiting for you in the warehouse. I'll finish up his rounds for him, which shouldn't take long, then meet you there. Not a word to anyone about this. After you've checked the place out, go ahead and call the local cops."

"Okay," Micah said. And that was that.

• • •

Jack Pense had retired from running an armored truck crew for Wackenhut Security ten years before. Too young for social security but with not enough income to support himself and his common-law wife, Jennifer Day, Jack had come to work for Cueball Boland's security firm a week after he was pensioned off.

During the drive to the warehouse on the back side of the Island, Micah summoned up an image of Jack's face—round, tired and somewhat pained. Mostly what he associated with him were a stack of read and re-read *Sackett* and *Longarm* novels and the stubs of chewed Muriel Magnum cigars. Also, he had known for years that Jack sometimes laced his on-the-job coffee with Southern Comfort and that he probably took too many pain pills, but who could blame him? Jack's ruptured discs and three fused vertebrae weren't imaginary. Jack's favorite topic was his injuries and his general health. He could be downright expansive on the subject. Aside from this, Micah's and Jack's conversations mainly kept to football, old western movies, and the antics of Depression era desperadoes such as Bonnie and Clyde, Raymond Hamilton, and Joe Palmer.

Micah had *liked* Jack Pense. Micah didn't like many people.

"Damn," he told the Island. It said nothing in return. It lay mocking and silent in the haze of the breaking dawn, a little exotic, a little seedy, and—as always—a little menacing. To his right and slightly over his shoulder, the sky and the horizon waters of the Gulf glowed with coming light while ahead loomed the grim, gray silhouette of the DeMour warehouse. "Damn," he said once again.

[3]

Micah Lanscomb and Cueball Boland had met five years earlier in a manner that in another time and in a more conventional place might have seemed strange. But Galveston is a port city, one with a threadbare allure many find irresistible. Its citizens are used to seeing the odd and the offbeat wash up on their shores.

Besides owning NiteWise Security, C.C. "Cueball" Boland was a pool hustler who operated his own billiards room a block off The Strand. Additionally, he was a retired Dallas cop who gambled moderately on poker, drank a fair amount of whiskey when the situation seemed to call for it (which it frequently did), and never failed to notice a pretty girl. Which is to say that he had all of the usual male vices and a couple he had cobbled together on his own. One vice he didn't have was philandering because his wife, the former Myrna Hutchins, had been the center of his erotic universe since sixth grade. Nor could he ever be accused of disloyalty to friends. It was this last quality that had gotten him into trouble several times since his retirement eight years earlier. Or as Myrna often said, "C.C. is the only man whose learning curve is a straight line."

Myrna said a lot of things like that, the kind of one-liners Groucho Marx would have appreciated. To his credit, Cueball listened to her. It was Myrna's dry wit and uncanny sense of proportion that had attracted him to her long before the raging hormones of his early teens took charge of him, body and soul. Over the years it was his sense of loyalty that gathered to him a smattering handful of long-time friends, those few who had proven equal to the engulfing depths of his devotion. Much later in life, one of those friends was Micah Lanscomb.

Micah came into Cueball's life from the rain, both literally and figuratively. Lanscomb was soaked, thin and weathered, and wore an impenetrable and taciturn demeanor. He was a head taller than his fellows and his shadow came before him, a palpable, inescapable thing that parted idle chatter like the wake of a great ship traversing middling waters. If the person meeting him were pressed on the matter, he would have said that the tall man was engaged in weighty matters, which, on the face of it, was the simple truth.

The pool hall was already quiet that fateful evening. The jukebox was being given its requisite thirty minutes to cool down, the plug disengaged and held against the wall by a racked billiard cue. The repairman who'd fixed the turntable motor and charged Cueball sixty bucks for the service call had advised a cooling down period each night—just one more thing Cueball could add to his religious regimen. It was either that or replace the damned thing, but Cueball had a soft place in his heart for old jukeboxes.

Outside the storm freshened, diminished, and came on once again with a howl. Then suddenly, like an apparition, a wet stranger appeared just inside the doorway, dripping on the bare wooden floors.

"Help you?" Cueball asked.

"I don't have any money," the stranger said, "but I'm hungry and I'll wash dishes and clean the place up to cover it."

Cueball closed his eyes and took a deep breath. When he turned and opened them again he saw his own reflection in the long mirror behind the bar—a nondescript gray man of sixty-two years with graying hair and a face that people found difficult to remember even when they were looking right at it. He was five ten and weighed a hundred and sixty-five pounds—neither tall nor short, neither stocky nor skinny. The clothes he wore were usually as unmemorable as the body they covered. A writer friend had once told him that there was something about him reminiscent of the flicker of old black-and-white film—quick celluloid images at the corner of an unfocused eye like those long-ago RKO newsreels from childhood afternoons spent at the quarter matinee.

He turned back to the man and stared at him. This was, beyond doubt, the kind of person he'd always resolutely, and with little success, sought to avoid—gaunt, hollow, needy, empty. A man like the thousands of others who wander this great and turbulent land looking for the one unnamable thing that might fill them, the undefined Holy Grail of their rootless existence. Yet there was a tiny something besides emptiness in the man's eyes—something that said there was a story there worth hearing. And Cueball Boland was a man who listened to stories.

Cueball shrugged. "Pete," he said quietly to the huge black man behind the bar. "Put a rib-eye on the grill and turn on the fryer. I do believe this poor guy could stand a square meal."

"Much obliged," the man said.

"Want a beer?" Cueball asked.

"Naw. A coke, maybe."

Cueball's hand had been resting on the cooler. He slid back the door, reached down and pulled up a bottle, maneuvered it under the church-key out of habit, his pale gray eyes locked with the stranger's. Cueball didn't bother to give the man a smile. The fellow was beyond caring about petty things.

The stranger took the coke and wandered over to a table, sat down and stared into the darkest corner of the room, oblivious. And so Cueball Boland went and joined him.

• • •

Micah Lanscomb's story would come out, fully told, over a five-year period. Over those years, it would take the better part of a full case of Johnnie Walker Black Label whiskey to coax it forth.

As Lanscomb's tale had it, in 1968 he'd left his family home in a dead end East Texas small town and made his way westward to San Francisco and the mecca of the children of Aquarius, the intersection of Haight Street with Ashbury. After weeks of hanging out with flower children, smoking dope from tall bongs between intermittent readings from Frodo's passage of Moria and Gandalf's consequent fall, he awoke one morning with the sure knowledge that his new hippie friends were full of shit to the precise degree they loudly clamored to be heard and understood. Which was not surprising given the fact they were, by-and-large, overgrown children, many of whom had been kicked from conservative nests as awkward and unfit offspring. It was, after all, a time of little understanding.

Experience was what Micah was looking for, experience with life and living. But in the cool California atmosphere of rebellion and irresponsibility there seemed little evidence that anyone else was on the same quest.

And so his quest turned inward. The drugs became harder drugs.

His first disaster came during a group campout on the beach at Malibu. He'd taken the ride down the Coast Highway with a busload of flower children in search of a score. During a particularly disturbing acid trip on the beach, one of the girls who had been traded around was murdered. Micah heard the screams in a starlit, acid-fueled darkness while wrestling with an eerie and ever-shifting reality. The stars overhead had become streaky, violent arcs. The sand beneath his bare feet sucked away at him as if drawing his life force downward from his heart. At first he thought the screeches were that of a peacock from the neighbor's yard back home and in his distant childhood, but soon they became something else entirely. By the time he gathered himself enough to launch forward to investigate, there was only the still and lifeless body, savaged and torn beneath the cold glare of a cheap flashlight. He hadn't loved her. No one had loved her, to his knowledge. And Micah Lanscomb hadn't saved her. She was as much Kitty Genovese as she had been Susan "Sun-energy" Glover of the long, willowy legs and blond, Galadriel tresses. And she was dead.

He walked away that night. Walked away from California.

Death very nearly found him in a jailhouse in a small Nevada desert town at the hands of a sheriff's deputy who didn't care to stomach his smell. The deputy had tried to use him for a punching bag. Micah took the blows one by one up to the moment he realized the man wasn't going to stop until his target ceased breathing. He then reached out two wiry arms past the deputy's flailing limbs, applied an exact amount of pressure to his carotid artery, and relieved the deputy of consciousness long enough to liberate himself from jail, town, and the sovereign State of Nevada.

Eastward he walked, over mountains and across plains. He swam rivers, camped out with the ragged flotsam of humanity, and stopped when the Atlantic lapped at his ankles. There being no place further to go, he came home to Texas.

Four years had passed in a twinkling. His father was dead and his mother had remarried and moved off to Ohio. The town of Wilford was a husk of its former self. The home place, a two-bedroom shotgun house, was still standing empty. He took up residence. Two weeks after he hit town, he got a job at the local jail. Within five years he was the county sheriff. The locals, insular and suspicious of what they, in this late day, still called "the laws," liked his diplomatic approach to law enforcement.

In 1979 he attended a symphony concert at Sam Houston State University, fifty miles away. The highlight was a Juilliard harpist named Diana Sulbee. He watched her from the first row, enchanted with her beauty and with the way she merged herself, body and soul, with the music that flowed as clear and crystalline as a cold mountain stream from her precious, slender fingers.

After the concert he went backstage, spoke to her briefly, and then surprised himself by asking her to dinner. Inexplicably, she accepted. They were married five days later before the Justice of the Peace in Wilford.

For two of the briefest and most beautiful years of his life, Micah Lanscomb was happy. That happiness was shattered when Diana was killed by an eighteen-wheel tractor-trailer rig whose driver failed to yield the right of way on an Interstate 45 feeder ramp and plowed over her sports car.

His wife's death was his penance, Micah felt, for having let Susan Glover die that dark California night all those years before.

After the funeral—which was the largest gathering ever seen in the isolated and insular little town—Micah handed his badge and his gun to his senior deputy and pressed the keys to his truck into the bronzed hands of the Mexican grave digger. Then he began walking, yet again. This time south.

Micah walked until he met ocean once more.

Below the Galveston seawall in the turbulent waters of the Gulf, he purged himself of everything, both ugly and beautiful, and very nearly drowned in the bargain when a rip-current pulled him further out to sea. But he knew, instinctively, anything good that comes must be paid for, and sometimes the price is dear.

The man who emerged from the waves and the rocks was a different man. A man finally at peace with himself. And it was that man upon whom Cueball Boland would, in carefully measured doses over the course of time, ladle out his trust and his devotion.

[4]

Jack Pense was murdered in a warehouse that belonged to the DeMour family. The DeMours were Old Island Money like the Moodys and the Kempners and the Sealys. In Galveston old money was quiet money—money that kept its own counsel in the shuttered mansions in the city's historic East End and in a few walnut-paneled boardrooms in the unprepossessing buildings within a couple of blocks of Broadway. Old Money in Galveston was Big Money. Micah knew that back in the fifties the Moody Bank, headquartered in its sedate five-story brick building on Market Street, held a mortgage on every Hilton hotel on the face of this round green Earth. Yet the vast majority of Americans had never even heard the name. People in Galveston liked it that way, that Old Money was both big and quiet. No one would be pleased that the killing occurred at the DeMour warehouse. It would bring light and attention where none were wanted.

It took only one look at Jack Pense's body for Micah to know what had happened. "Man, oh man," Rusty Taylor said. "Why would somebody *do* that? Could've been *me*, you know." Rusty was the rounds guard. He drove a little Daihatsu pickup truck from site to site, checking on things, making sure there were no open doors or bashed-in windows. Cueball had a definite policy about checking on his stationary guards. The rounds guard had to verify by sight the safety of every stationary guard on each round, which was how Rusty had found Jack's body.

"I know it could have been you, Rusty," Micah said, "but it wasn't. Go get yourself a cup of coffee. You're going to be awake for the next five or six hours at least."

"For what?" Rusty asked.

Micah turned and looked at the man and decided not to be sarcastic, which had become increasingly difficult as the years drifted on by. "You're going to have to answer the same set of questions fifty times, is why."

"Oh," Rusty said. But before he turned away he asked the question again, only differently. "Why would anybody breaking in to rob the place, kill the security guard after tying him up? Doesn't make any sense is all."

"Because whoever did it knew him."

Rusty shivered. "Oh," he said, and walked away.

Micah Lanscomb turned and regarded the mortal remains of Jack Pense.

Jack's face was a mass of bruises and contusions. It barely resembled him. He had been pummeled with either a tire iron or a stick of some kind. That would be the coroner's job to figure out. Jack's chest, what Micah could see of it through his torn shirt, was one massive bruise. The instrument of torture was not apparent at the scene.

The body was hours cold. Micah did a quick estimate and placed Jack's death sometime between three and four a.m. Between the autopsy findings and Rusty's shift report, that figure would likely be narrowed down.

Micah turned away from Jack Pense's body. His eyes came to rest on a desk by the loading dock. This was where Jack filled out his own shift report every night. It was where he drank his coffee, where he set out from on his rounds of the warehouse on those nights when his back wasn't giving him fits and he felt good enough to stretch his legs. In the dead of night when the place was all quiet, you could hear every sound made in the building from Jack's desk.

Jack's thermos was there next to the phone. Micah lifted a handkerchief out of his shirt pocket, spread it across his hand and lifted the thermos. With the other hand he brought up a corner of the cloth, covered the lid and twisted it open.

Micah sniffed then smiled.

"Good old Jack," he said and took a drink.

The coffee, laced as it was with a healthy dose of Irish Cream, went down just fine, even though it was now lukewarm. For good measure, he downed the rest of it in one long chug.

Micah turned and looked back toward the body.

"God bless you, Jackie Pense," he said. "Thanks for the drink. Now rest in peace, old son."

• • •

Micah placed the 911 call. After he hung up, he knew he had five minutes, tops, to make a quick inspection of the warehouse to determine if anything had been rifled, broken into, or stolen. He knew that dock employees would begin arriving at any time. He left the lifeless body of Jack Pense where Rusty had found him and made a slow transit around the warehouse.

He was dwarfed by pallets of freight stacked up to forty feet, shrink-wrapped like ancient Egyptian mummies—truck and tractor parts, whole loads of lawnmowers just in from Japan and Malaysia. They made for aisle after aisle of hard consumables and big-boy toys.

At the end of the aisle a flight of narrow wooden stairs led upward into the gloom. A door stood open at the top, revealing a deep well of darkness beyond.

"Now that's not right," Micah said aloud. He felt a chill then.

He had no more than a few minutes before the cops would arrive. If he hustled, maybe he'd have enough time to check it out and report to Cueball before they came.

[5]

Galveston police lieutenant Leland Morgan was annoyed but not surprised—annoyed because Boland's people had called their boss first, annoyed too that Boland had sent that Lanscomb clown over before he called the P.D. But he was not surprised because he knew that Cueball had been a cop himself. And you can't teach an old dog any new tricks.

Cueball Boland was on site when Morgan arrived. Jack Pense's body was being rolled out to the ambulance. It would go to Houston and the state forensics lab for an autopsy. Morgan looked toward the back of the warehouse. Boland was leaning against the rear wall. Morgan walked over to meet him.

"Tell me how you figure in this deal," he said.

Boland gave him a jaundiced look. "My guard was killed here. My employee."

"And?"

"The DeMour family owns three warehouses on the island. Besides doing their security, I'm their property manager. But you already knew that, didn't you?"

"Sure," he said. "I already knew that." Morgan was a tall, slim, middle-aged man with a smooth face and steely eyes. He tried to fix Boland with one of the patented stares he'd copied from Clint Eastwood movies, stares that had proven effective on those occasions when the suspect he was interviewing wasn't too bright. But in this instance, he felt his eyes blinking in spite of himself.

"Then why not cut the crap, Morgan? You can't pull anything on me I haven't used myself a thousand times before."

"I don't know," the man said thoughtfully. "Instinct, I guess. You know, I should like you better than I do since you're an ex-cop and all. And I should trust you more too. But I don't. Never have."

"Remind me to grieve over that when I have time," Cueball said easily.

"Yeah, right. How about this Pense guy?"

Cueball shrugged. "A very good hand. Dependable, trustworthy."

"What's his background?"

"Jack was born on the island. The family moved to Houston when he was young. He retired from a high-stress security company in Houston because of a back injury, but he couldn't make it on disability and came to me for a sit-down job, which is what he was doing for me mostly. I had him working with a younger man who's the rounds officer. Jack had a good record. He had no allegations of theft or excessive force. He was a low-key kind of guy who wasn't averse to using a little diplomacy. Smart enough, but uneducated. He used a lot of painkillers because of the back thing, but I never saw that they affected his judgment."

"So you knowingly hired a drug addict as a security officer?"

Cueball decided he was getting enough of this fool. "No, asshole, I knowingly hired a good man who was up front about his pain problems and his prescription drug use."

Morgan's already pale face went white. "You push it, don't you? Talking that way to a cop, I mean?"

Cueball gave him a cold smile. "I've got a special Texas Ranger commission in my pocket right now, so it's one cop talking to another. If you don't like my style of expression, complain to your local senator. Or maybe the governor. They're both good friends."

Morgan made a sour face and nodded. "So that's how it is, huh? Friends in Austin?"

"No. Old friends downtown here in Galveston, which amounts to the same thing."

Morgan wheezed a little and changed tack. "Who rents the warehouse from the DeMours?"

"Gulfway Discount Stores. You're familiar with them, right?"

Morgan nodded. "Yeah. A straight-up outfit, as far as I know. What about Pense's family?"

"His parents are dead, but he has a live-in girlfriend. Micah can give you her name and address. I'll have Myrna photocopy Pense's employment file for you. Believe it or not, we're on the same side here. I'm not hiding anything. Aside from the fact that this is bad for my business, Pense was a decent guy, and I take it personally."

"Good enough. I'll send somebody over to your house this afternoon to get it."

"One more thing," Boland said.

"Yeah?"

"Now that you know I have friends where a man needs them, it might be wise of you to cultivate me a little. I may be able to open some doors you can't. I'm not suggesting that you should kiss my ass. Just a little courtesy and benefit of the doubt would do."

Morgan regarded him thoughtfully for a few moments, then said, "Something to think about. You know, Boland, you're not the only person with Island connections."

"That's right. I remember now. It seems to me Vivian DeMour helped get you promoted to lieutenant, didn't she?"

"Now how the hell would you know that?"

"I know everything that happens on this island," Cueball said. "Now, what about my warehouse?"

"You can let authorized people in as the need arises. Keep the immediate crime area taped off and people out of it. Other than that, business as usual. This had to be personal. Nobody killed this guy to steal a pallet full of lawn mowers."

"I don't think so either," Boland said.

• • •

Cueball watched Morgan walk away. He waited until the cop's city-issue Ford Crown Victoria was gone from sight before reaching into his back pocket for his radio. He keyed the mic. "Micah. You there?"

"Here, boss," Micah's slow drawl came back to him over the air.

"Any of the cops still in that room?" Cueball asked.

"Nope."

"Alright. Lock it down tight then. I'm going to dust that damned safe myself and lift any prints that turn up."

"And do what with them?"

"I'm going to have a friend in the Bureau up in Houston run anything I find through the national fingerprint database."

"What about Morgan?" Micah asked. "Do you plan to tell him?"

"Eventually."

"Are you going to tell me what this is all about?"

"Sure, but not right now. I've got to think it through first."

"So start thinking," Micah said.

"I will. You go break the news to Jenny."

"I get all the fun stuff, huh?"

Cueball sighed and felt a little ashamed of himself. "I don't relish seeing women cry. But I do plan on going to the funeral home with her tomorrow. I imagine I'll have to be the one who winds up paying for Jack's funeral service. But for now, I want you to be the one to tell Jenny. You were closer to Jack than I was. Later, she'll be glad it came from you."

• • •

The sun was two hours above the horizon when Micah knocked quietly on the door to the apartment Jack Pense shared with Jennifer Day. It was all Jenny's place now, and Jack's meager belongings were hers.

She didn't cry when he told her. Instead she looked at Micah Lanscomb with shocked, baby-blue eyes. Her face went stony and her jaws clenched together like a pair of vice-grips straining at their tolerance point. Then she did the complete opposite of what Micah had imagined. She turned, sat down on the sofa with a defeated sigh and turned off the television with the remote. "Could you make us a pot of coffee, Micah?" she asked in a soft nasal voice that made her sound like a little girl.

Galveston, Texas

OCTOBER 1943

[6]

Longnight never knew why he chose the Texas Coast. Not that he cared. Nor did he know why he chose Galveston, but as it turned out it was a perfect choice. He had recovered his money less than a week after staging an escape from the clinic. It was in a bus station storage locker he'd rented when he began to suspect the government might be close behind him—the last vestige of his inheritance, a cool seventy thousand dollars. It had been good thinking to stash it away somewhere safe. The Ohio murders had made national headlines, and he'd gotten himself caught. But then the Feds had found his research notes in his apartment, the Army had stepped in and he had been moved to Virginia and put in with the loonies.

His car, a very clean two-year-old Packard convertible coupe, had been purchased in Memphis. In Little Rock he picked up an expensive elk hide suitcase at a department store and three off-the-rack suits in one of the town's better men's shops. He also bought a shaving kit, some other needed toiletries, several white dress shirts and a dozen pair of underwear. He spent the night in Texarkana, not bothering to sample the delights of the town's famous bordellos. The next morning he was up early and on the road. He pulled into Beaumont at a little past two in the afternoon and drove around a little, getting the feel of the town. It was not to his liking.

After a quick lunch, he drove along the coast to the west, stopping only when the highway came to a dead end at a big sign that said "Galveston Ferry." He had heard of the town and found the name intriguing. The wait for the ferry was only about five minutes, and the ride over to the Island but a couple of miles. When the boat docked, he drove off and followed the road across a narrow strip of barren land that marked the eastern extremity of the island. The road dead-ended at a broad, four-lane street that was named Seawall Boulevard. He turned right. A mile and a half later, almost as if by instinct, he pulled up in front of the great Hotel Galvez, the town's most regal hostelry.

He checked in under Randall Talos, a phony name, and slipped the desk clerk a five to get a small suite at the front of the building overlooking the Gulf. The desk clerk rang the bell and a young Negro bellhop of perhaps fifteen appeared from around the corner and began helping him with his bags.

On the way up the elevator, Longnight made it a point to get the bellhop's name: Tad Blessing.

Up in his fifth floor room, he gave another five to the bellhop and said, "Where's the action, Tad?"

Tad Blessing was a brash-looking kid with a quick manner and a feral gleam in his eye. The kid didn't even bother to size his guest up. Galveston was that kind of town. "What kind of action you want?" he asked. "Women? Gamblin'?"

"Maybe later on the women."

"Well, if you do need some female company, Post Office Street is the place. There's some fine lookin' girls on Post Office Street. Some really nice houses there. If you don't want to leave your room, just have the desk clerk send me up and I can have one of the ladies come and visit a spell."

"I may do it. How about the gambling?"

The kid took him by the arm and led him to the window and pointed directly across the street to a large building situated at the end of a pier that stretched a hundred yards or so out over the Gulf. "Ya see that?"

"Yeah. I wondered what it was when I drove up."

"That there is the Balinese Room. Finest nightspot between Brownsville and Miami."

"Really?"

"Yeah. That enclosed catwalk makes it awful tough to raid—not that anybody's gonna to be trying to raid it. There's a trinket shop in the land end of the catwalk, and that's where you have to get approved. No problem. Just wear a tie and coat or a tux and you can get into the nightclub without any problem. Artie Shaw and his band are playin' there this week. Sinatra was there a month or so ago."

"How about the gambling?"

The kid shrugged. "The casino is in back of the nightclub. Last room out over the water. But it'll be tougher to get into. Act reasonable and don't push it if they say no. That could be...dangerous. Just come back again the next night and ask all over again. Quietly keep at it, that's the ticket. It'll help a little if you tell 'em you're staying here at the Galvez."

"Is the casino honest?" he asked the kid.

The kid laughed a cynical little laugh. "What's honest? The odds is so much in favor of the house in casino gambling that only fools would cheat. But there's no rigged tables or shaved dice or any of that crap at the Balinese Room."

"Who runs it?"

"The Maceo brothers."

The name was vaguely familiar to the man. He nodded and slipped the kid a couple more bucks.

The boy smiled and said, "If you want something, call downstairs and ask for me."

He riveted the boy with his eyes and spoke in a silky voice that held a hint of challenge. "About sending that girl up...Are you a pimp, Tad? Is that how you think of yourself?"

The kid laughed again, and this time it was an honest laugh, one free of cynicism. "It's a rough world, and a fellah's got to get by. So I just think of myself as whatever I need to be whenever I need to be it."

The man winked. "I feel exactly the same way. How about bringing me up a bottle of good Canadian whiskey and some ice?"

"Sure 'nough."

"I'll be in the bath. Just set it on the table and we'll settle up tomorrow. Will that do?"

"Right as rain."

"You're a good lad, Mr. Blessing," he said with a hearty laugh. "May your life be long and prosperous."

• • •

He dressed with care, donning one of his white dress shirts, a tie of mottled gold and burgundy, and a dark blue double-breasted suit of all-weight worsted wool pinstripe. He turned off all the lights except for one small table lamp and sat beside it enjoying a whiskey over ice. At precisely eight he arose and left the room. Down in the lobby he paused for a moment to take a single white carnation from the bouquet on the grand piano. Out in the street he threaded the carnation's stem into his lapel. He crossed the street.

An older couple came up to the door of the catwalk just as he approached. He swept the door open for them and stood to one side. As they entered, they smiled gratefully and nodded their thanks. What they saw was a tall, slim, handsome man with brown hair, a shy smile, and a diffident manner, which was exactly what he wanted them to see.

Before he followed, he took one last deep breath of the cool air, relishing the salty, earthy odor of the island. He looked around him. Far out on the Gulf, hundreds of lights glittered where vessels from half the nations of the earth stretched to the horizon, riding the swells, each awaiting its entry to the Houston ship channel. Heavy cars whisked up and down the street, stopping to let out their richly dressed passengers at the casinos and nightclubs that dotted the seawall. The soft strains of Shaw's *Begin the Beguine* drifted out above a moonlit beach while palm trees rustled softly in the gentle breeze. Could there be a more glamorous time and place? He thought not. The whole world was mad with war, and the night was alive with promise. He might have a few glasses of champagne. He might strike up an interesting conversation. He might even come across an alluring young woman who wanted to dance. He might...

He smiled happily and walked down the catwalk toward the famed Balinese Room.

• *Galveston, Texas*

OCTOBER 1987

[7]

The beaten and lifeless body of Jack Pense. A grieving woman. An opened office that should have been locked. An opened safe which, according to Vivian DeMour, the last remaining member of the family to carry the name, contained nothing of real importance and never had.

These things troubled Micah Lanscomb, but what made it so much worse was how Jack Pense's death had clearly affected Cueball Boland. If it affected Cueball, there were clear ramifications for Galveston Island. Not that Cueball was the most important man on the Island. He was, however, one of the two most important personages in Micah Lanscomb's own personal pantheon, a distinction Cueball shared only with Myrna Boland, a woman Micah would easily lay down his life to protect.

That evening Micah went over to Cueball's house, a stately old Queen Anne Victorian on Ball Street in the East End. It was their Tuesday night custom to get together for a few drinks after Micah had made the deposit from the day's pool hall and bar proceeds. They sat on the front porch and sipped Johnnie Walker Black Label and tried to get a handle on things. In the dark fronds of the palm trees, an orchestra of cicadas was tuning up for the long night.

Myrna appeared and poured half a glass of Johnnie Walker for each of them but took the bottle back inside with her, as if to say "You can have this much, boys, but no more."

When she was gone, Cueball asked, "What are you thinking?"

"You don't want to know," Micah said.

"That's alright. I'll tell you what you were thinking, seeing as how I know you so well. You're thinking it was one of my own employees or former employees, aren't you? You've been clutching at the idea like a goddamned south sea islander clutches his kona doll ever since you entered old Dave DeMour's office."

"Maybe I have," Micah said. "Who else could it have been?"

Cueball took a sip of scotch and leaned back in Myrna's wicker settee. "I got the prints back from Washington two hours ago," Cueball said. "Those boys work quickly."

"Well, who the hell do they belong to?"

"To the one person I thought they'd belong to when I heard Jack Pense was found murdered while on duty."

Micah waited.

"I had the chance to kill the son of bitch who did it twenty years ago up in Dallas. A warehouse, a murder, and a safe. They all point to one man, and the fingerprints confirm it. A con named Harrison Lynch."

"I've heard of him," Micah said. "So how does he figure into this mess?"

"He's Jack Pense's stepbrother."

"Damn!"

Cueball nodded. "It's an old island story, full of rumor and supposition, but the accepted version is that Lindy—one of the DeMour daughters and my old friend Vivian's sister—got herself pregnant around age fifteen. That wasn't what you'd call socially acceptable back then, and it wasn't ordinarily discussed. The family tried to keep it a secret but the child was kidnapped and disappeared just as if it were dead. The kid reappeared years later as part of the Pense family, a lesser but still Old Island family who had moved to Houston."

Cueball paused for a moment, thinking. "The Penses moved to Houston after the patriarch lost his money. Later, he apparently lost his mind and killed himself. Harrison Lynch never even knew he was related to the DeMours until much later. The story goes that Harrison was a mean little shit from the day he was whelped. There was no love lost between him and the Pense family. Jack was a straight arrow and Harrison was always in trouble. Jack got the good grades while Harrison alternated between flunking courses and getting two-week expulsions. Then he went from bad to worse and left town. Somewhere along the way Harrison got in a mess out in West Texas, jumped bond, and finally wound up killing a couple of people, one in Dallas and one in Houston."

"They sent him up for life, right?" Micah asked.

Cueball shook his head and drained his glass in one long pull. "Not initially. He got two death penalties, but the Supreme Court moratorium on executions automatically commuted his sentences."

"How long has he been out?" Micah asked, and followed suit with his own glass.

"From the Dreyfus Unit the other side of Houston? Since yesterday morning," Cueball said.

[8]

After standing in on a night shift for Rusty Taylor—who, as Micah had predicted, spent an entire day at the Galveston police station and needed his rest—Micah took a drive down to the seawall in the company truck. It was six and the sun was a golden ball suspended over the Gulf. There was no traffic. It was his favorite time of day. He stopped in for breakfast at a little diner called Nell's only to find a message waiting for him. He crossed the street and went down one of the narrow stairways to the beach.

He shucked his boots, cut across the sand with them over his shoulder, got to the edge of the surf and started walking east. Bits of detritus—sand dollars, small shells, driftwood—littered the beach. Micah walked until he found Homer Underwood. Homer was a beachcomber and an alcoholic. He was probably a drug addict to boot, but Micah loved the crusty old son-of-a-bitch.

"Hey, Homer. I got a message that you needed to see me. Let me buy you breakfast."

"Ahhh! Micah! You can just give me a fiver. I'll get my own breakfast with it."

"Homer, if I give you five bucks, you'll drink it. It's too early for booze anyway. Come on. We're not far from Nell's. She'll make us a couple eggs and some sausages."

Homer took off his baseball cap, looked out to sea and scratched his head.

"You want information. I knew you'd be hunting me up anyway, that's why I left the message."

"I want to buy you breakfast too. It's my duty in life to make sure you eat at least once a week."

"Naw," Homer shook his head slowly. "Nope. Your duty is to find the man who killed Jack Pense. That's what you're about. Ain't it?"

Micah looked at the old man, gauging him. A slow smile spread across Micah's face. He couldn't help it. "Yeah," he said. "I can't fool you, Homer. But you asked me to look you up."

"It'll cost you," Homer said. "We just left downtown Small-change-ville and we're headed for C-note City. Ain't we?"

Micah pulled out his wallet, opened it, fished for a hundred and handed it to Homer. The old man took it, studied it for a minute, then handed it back to Micah.

"What's the matter?" Micah asked.

"I changed my mind about taking your money for this. I think I'll take that breakfast instead."

• • •

Nell's had gone through a number of conversions over the years. To hear Cueball tell it, it had been the island's first coin-op laundry back when he was a kid. A nickel a wash, if you could believe it. Sometime back in the seventies it became a seashell and surfboard shop: a true tourist trap. For the last ten years or so, it had enjoyed the distinction of being first a doughnut shop, then a sandwich place, and most recently a plain old-fashioned diner. There were four tables inside and two small, salt-air weathered tables of wrought iron and gray wood outside under the short overhang. Whenever Micah fed Homer Underwood at Nell's, they ate outside. Nell wouldn't hear of having the old varmint sit and eat inside her establishment. He wasn't exactly right for the image she wanted to convey.

Homer wolfed his food and Micah tried not to watch. When he was done, Homer wiped his mouth with his weather-stained shirttail and sighed deeply.

"Got a cigarette?" he asked.

"Nope. Sorry, old buddy."

"That's fine. That's fine."

"So what do you have for me?"

Homer Underwood looked off for a few moments, seemingly in deep thought. Then he turned back and fixed Micah with his bright old eyes. "I do know something," he said. "And let's just say I know more than is strictly healthy for me, or you, or just about anybody."

"I'm listening to you, Homer. I'm hangin' on every word."

"Harrison Lynch."

For a moment Micah felt like he'd been hit in the head with a big rubber hammer. "What makes you mention that name?"

"I may be an old fool, but sometimes I do read the paper. I've got newsprint in my blood, if you didn't know. Last week I read about Lynch's upcoming release."

"Go on..."

"Micah, how old would you say I am?"

"Oh, I don't know, Homer. 'Bout fifty-five? Sixty?"

Homer leaned back in his chair and put his hands up on his balding, sun-baked pate. "Almost seventy. I was born in 1917. I've lived on this island all my life. I've ridden out every hurricane that's come along. Never evacuated a single time no matter what those assholes at the weather service said. I was here back when World War II ended. I remember that every fire truck in town, every police siren, every church bell and every car-horn was wailin' or ringin' or honkin' on VJ-Day. But before that, in the late fall of '43 something hit this town and it wasn't no hurricane."

"Fall of '43?"

"You ain't old enough to remember. Let me tell it and don't steal my thunder."

"Sure, Homer," Micah said.

"As I was saying, *late* fall of '43. November and December. There was a big bunch of killings here on the island. Eleven deaths that are known about, and that was in a month's time. One every three days on an average and there could have been more."

"Eleven."

"Like I say, there could have been more. There was some evidence that a few of the victims were hacked up and fed to the crabs off the South Jetty. There were some transients and winos and what-not who turned up missing, but you know how that goes. Eleven were found for sure, mostly women. The killer started by cleaning out a whole bordello, all the girls including the owner, then began picking off the odd Post Office Street whore now and again. Not too long after that he started killing wholesale. Now you might find it hard to believe that a bunch of killings like that never made the national headlines. But please remember that, first, we were at war. With the war on, the whole country was looking the other way, you know. Second, Galveston at that time was the Riviera of the Gulf Coast. The town needed the business and that kind of press wasn't welcome. It's amazing to me that it still never got out, even though I—well, I was a reporter back then."

"Yeah. I remember somebody telling me that. They said you used to be something."

"I'm still something, although I don't know what. Anyway, those killings would have made a good story. It sure would have."

"Yeah?"

"Yeah."

Homer Underwood paused in his eating for a moment. He leaned back and looked out the plate glass window to the deep azure blue of the Gulf beyond. The old man had a somber look about him, as if he were looking for something he'd lost.

"And?"

Micah found that he was leaning forward—straining, in fact. He purposefully took a deep breath and leaned back in his chair and waited.

"I was thinking of someone from back then. It's someone you'll have to look into."

"Who was it?"

"Denny Muldoon. He was an FBI agent back in the day."

"Muldoon. All right. I'll remember."

"While you're checking into him, there was another fellow around back then. A Texas Ranger named Bonaparte Foley. Mean as a rattlesnake, that one."

"I've heard of him," Micah said. "I'm pretty sure Foley is dead."

"Yeah. Foley's dead, but I don't know about Muldoon. He...he might be. So by now you're asking yourself what a serial killer from forty plus years ago has to do with a warehouse killing from a couple of nights ago. That's exactly what you have to find out."

Micah laughed and Homer flicked a look at him and smiled. Micah realized Homer must have once been quite a handsome man.

"You wouldn't want me to make things too easy for you, now would you?" Homer asked.

"Of course not."

"Well, I think I've said enough."

Micah nodded.

Homer prodded his remaining bits of food with a fork then set the fork down. "You know, I've worked this island. I've lived it. I'll die this island. And I'm telling you this just once. Little Jacky Pense didn't die over money or drugs or nothing stupid like that. Now in your mind you're looking for a born loser named Harrison Lynch because he was Jack Pense's stepbrother, or so the story went."

"But Homer, how do you—"

"All I'm saying is, you take the less-traveled path and you might get somewhere. But finding Harrison Lynch and not going any further is the broad highway straight to hell and nowhere. You find out who Harrison Lynch *really* is. That's your ticket, old son. Because if I'm right in what I think, Jack Pense isn't going to be the last killing."

"What do you mean by that?" Micah asked intently.

Homer shrugged. "There was a lot of speculation that went on back in those days, and a lot of it was whispered. Vague rumors and half-told tales. You dig them up and I believe you'll be getting somewhere. And now that's all I'm going to say. I've said too damn much as it is."

"Okay. One last question," Micah said. "What does Bonaparte Foley have to do with this whole mess?"

"He was the ranger sent down here to put a stop to the killings. By hook or crook."

"What do you mean, by hook or—"

"That's how things sometimes worked back then. Foley was supposed to find the guy and make the case on him. But if he couldn't make a solid case, he was supposed punch his ticket for him."

"Did he find him?"

The old man laughed a grim little laugh. "Well, the killings stopped and there never was any prosecution, so you figure it out. Now that's all you're getting from me."

"All right," Micah said, and meant it. "I won't press you any further." He opened his wallet and handed the old man the hundred-dollar bill. Homer took it without hesitation. Maybe he'd already forgotten that he'd turned it down.

• • •

When Micah got back to his truck, he found a ticket for illegal parking under one of the wiper blades, flapping in the gulf breeze. On the signature line printed in perfectly legible block letters was the name of the officer who had issued it: Leland Morgan. The son-of-a-bitch even put an exclamation point after his name.

[9]

Lieutenant Leland Morgan watched Micah Lanscomb as he walked along the beach below the seawall. It was low tide at the moment, and the strip of beach had widened by perhaps a hundred yards. Lanscomb had his boots over his shoulder and seemed to be in no hurry. His patrol uniform was rumpled, his overly-long hair flopped around in the breeze. There was no telling what Boland saw in the guy. How could he trust him so implicitly with his business?

The beach was otherwise deserted at this hour. It was just Lanscomb and the surf. Morgan had to climb back inside his cruiser at one point when Lanscomb disappeared from view past a hotel boardwalk. He drove a quarter of a mile down. He passed the boardwalk and parked opposite the hotel that stood over the water on top of a forest of black pilings. He got out and approached the seawall, walked a few yards on the wide boardwalk, and watched Lanscomb.

Lanscomb had stopped and was looking toward a set of stairs ahead of him that ascended from the beach to the top of the seawall. Morgan waited and fingered his binoculars.

A man came into view from the stairs and sauntered across the sand toward Lanscomb. It was the beachcomber—Underwood.

Underwood approached Lanscomb and the two began talking. Morgan raised his binoculars.

"What are you two dipshits saying?" Morgan whispered under his breath. "Goddammit, I better let her know right away."

Morgan watched as Lanscomb pulled out his wallet and offered money to Underwood, who appeared to refuse it. Lanscomb then gestured back the way he had come—in the direction of Nell's.

A shiver went up Morgan's spine. If they turned, they would certainly see him. At this angle, if he moved, the motion might attract their attention.

Leland Morgan stepped back slowly across the boardwalk until his tailbone encountered the opposite railing. He crouched until only the top of his head could be seen from the vantagepoint of the two men.

At that moment the two turned toward him and began walking.

Morgan waited until they were beneath him, thirty feet down, then stood and walked back to his cruiser. He drove to Nell's, where Lanscomb's little security truck was parked illegally by the seawall. He stopped next to the truck and a smile slowly spread across his face.

It took no more than a moment to write the parking citation. He had to fish through his glove box for the pad, though. It had been more than a year since he'd written a ticket. It was something a lieutenant didn't normally do but technically *could*. He paused only a moment when he had filled out the form down to the officer's signature line. Normally, his signature was no more than an illegible scrawl. It was the badge number next to it that the municipal court went by in the event the violator pled not guilty and he'd have to appear before the bench or a jury. Instead, Morgan wrote his name in plain block letters. He wanted Lanscomb to know his place in the scheme of things, and who was putting him there.

The breeze from the Gulf drove the odor of salt spray into his sinuses. He fought the urge to sneeze.

Why the hell was he here in Galveston, so far from Lubbock and home?

Leland Morgan shook his head. For some questions there weren't any answers.

He placed the ticket under the wiper blade of Lanscomb's pickup, climbed back into his cruiser and drove away, his spirits beginning to lift for a change.

[10]

The DPS lab completed the autopsy and sent Jack Pense's body back to Galveston shortly after noon. C.C. Boland had Jennifer Day clutching his arm when he walked into the Welch and Sons Funeral Home to make the arrangements.

Billy Welch, the owner of half a dozen funeral chapels strung along the Texas Gulf Coast, was there to greet them. Billy's sleeves were rolled up and he was ready to help. Billy and C.C. had known each other since the two of them were kids in grade school.

Jenny picked out a five-thousand dollar casket, the flowers and the headstone. Billy tried to shave the price downward, knowing it was one of Cueball's employees, but Cueball glanced at the figures and shook his head.

"What the hell you think you're trying to do, Billy?"

"What do you mean?" Welch asked.

C.C. sighed and fished out his checkbook. "You're undercharging me, and you're doing it on purpose." Then he wrote a check for a little over seven thousand dollars and never batted an eye. He placed the check in Billy's hand and Welch sighed deeply.

"Thank you, C.C.," he said. And meant it.

After the arrangements were made, Billy requested a two-hour window to prep the body for a brief viewing. It would be a closed casket ceremony—this Cueball had known, having already seen the grisly remains at the warehouse—but Jack's common-law wife hadn't seen him yet.

During the wait, Cueball took Jenny to a cafeteria a block down from the funeral home and made it a point to get her a cup of coffee and spike it with Irish rum. Business was slow. The two were seated alone in a section away from the listless cafeteria workers. Every time Jenny got her spiked cup of java drank halfway down, C.C. reached across and poured in another dollop of rum from his flask. At her first protestation, Cueball said, "This will stiffen your spine a little. And you'll need it when you go in and see Jacky." And so she drank and drank some more. Just about the time Cueball estimated she was feeling no pain, his pager beeped.

Cueball read the number, got up and used the pay phone in the lobby. Micah answered on the first ring.

"Did you know a Texas Ranger by the name of Foley?" Micah sounded perpetually tired.

"Of course I knew him. In fact, I was at his funeral, along with the most of the rangers in the state."

"Okay. Good."

"What's Foley got to do with this?" Cueball asked.

"Uh. Let's just say I have my sources. Maybe we should be looking for a little more than just Harrison Lynch."

"Yeah? Who's your source?"

"It's—"

"Huh! I already know. It's Homer Underwood, isn't it? Why do you listen to that old grifter?"

"He's no grifter, Cueball. At least not anymore. He's just an old man who knows things."

"Alright. Fine. And Homer knew Lynch was involved?"

"He mentioned the name before I did," Micah replied.

"What else did he say? And how did Foley figure into his thinking?"

"Homer said he suspected that Jack's death tied into a bunch of killings that happened here back during the war. Foley worked the case. In fact, according to Homer, Foley was sent down here to put a stop to the murders by whatever means necessary."

"Which war?" Cueball asked.

"*The* war. World War II."

Micah Lanscomb heard a very long roar of nothing over the line and waited. Finally Cueball spoke. "Alright. Have you slept yet?"

"No. I'm not tired."

"That's because you burned that fuse out a long time ago. All right, these are orders: Go home and get some sleep. Drop by the house tonight, though, and I'll tell you about Harrison Lynch."

"Okay, but what about Foley? And the other fellow Homer named? Denny Muldoon?"

"Muldoon? Don't know him. What about them?" Cueball asked.

Micah laughed. "I suppose we'll talk about it tonight."

"Get some sleep. You sound like the walking dead."

Cueball heard the phone click dead and snorted. "Well, hell," he said to himself.

When Cueball returned to the table he found Jennifer snoring softly. He woke her and they went back to the funeral home and completed the arrangements. The funeral was to be two days hence.

[11]

"You promised to tell me the story of Harrison Lynch," Micah said. They sat on the front porch of Cueball's house, just as they had so many times before, enjoying the balmy darkness of the Gulf night.

"You know, in a couple of weeks we'll have to move these sessions inside," Cueball said. "It's about to get too cool for late evening reveries."

"Lynch, Cueball! Quit evading the subject."

Boland laughed. "Where to start? Okay. I'd been on the force a year up in Dallas, but I was still a rookie by the old timers' standards. It was my first week in a radio car all on my own when the call came in..."

• • •

Cueball talked and Micah listened.

According to Cueball, Harrison Lynch was a slim character with a shock of wavy blond hair, a hatchet-shaped face, and a pair of teal blue eyes that were devoid of any trace of humanity. In a word, Harrison looked hungry.

His first recorded professional foray into his career as a thief was a motel burglary off the feeder road to Interstate 20 on the outskirts of Pecos, Texas. The year was 1966, and Harrison was a mere twenty-two years old. The official incident report stated that the thief came in through a hole in the roof of the attached tool shed. He got through a steel door by using a hand-drill through the lock mechanism and into the room containing the motel safe.

The motel manager was known to begin drinking early in the afternoon and to lock up the place as soon as the sun dipped below the horizon. Then he would polish off whatever bottle with which he happened to be engaged, and pass out somewhere in the vicinity of his cot—any actual bed to be had having been employed for the sole use of the guests, should there be any.

The safe contained a week's worth of receipts in the form of cash and traveler's checks totaling $762—a remarkable sum for a run-down motel slap dab in the middle of hell-and-gone. This total, however, would be significant for Harrison Lynch. It was twelve dollars over the minimum limit for a felony conviction. The local prosecutor, a former washout from the Mercury Astronaut Program, was more than ready to nail Lynch to the wall.

Lynch was bonded out of jail by his family—the Penses—and removed from Pecos for good long before the trial was to begin.

He put in an appearance in Houston three weeks later when he burgled a downtown jewelry store in the middle of a hot summer night. The take was seventy thousand in diamonds, gold, watches, necklaces, and a small stack of St. Gaudens twenty-dollar gold pieces. Harrison was moving up in the world.

During his second heist in Houston, Harrison Lynch killed his first human being. This was three weeks after the gold and jewels had been siphoned through the network of black beer and whiskey joints that kept Houston's Fifth Ward juiced and throbbing, converted to hard cash and spent on prostitutes of every ilk. His victim was an elderly night watchman, a black man, who came upon Harrison after he fell from the roof of a warehouse that stood along the Houston Ship Channel.

It was a hot, humid night in high summer during the dark of the moon. The night man, a sixty-six-year-old grandfather named Curtis Gray, heard the racket and the moaning and went to investigate. When he tried to help Harrison to his feet, Harrison pulled a knife and stabbed the man five times in the belly and once in the throat, then whined like a baby for twenty minutes over his scraped knee. When he finally pulled himself together, he took Gray's keys and helped himself into the warehouse where he set off an alarm that caused permanent damage to both his ears. Harrison gained a set of keys, lost a knife and a good part of his hearing. It took Curtis Gray five days to die.

After the fingerprints were lifted from the knife, photographed and run through the FBI's Houston crime lab, both the Houston Police and the Texas Rangers became interested in the whereabouts of Harrison Lynch.

Within days the mug shot from his booking at the Pecos County Jail appeared on WANTED posters in every post office and police station throughout the Southwest.

Harrison was arrested two months later.

It was the middle of the night. Cueball Boland responded to an alarm call at a storage facility near the newly-constructed North Central Expressway. He cut his red and blue lights three blocks away from the call, killed his headlights and coasted up to the place by feel in the close dark.

The manager, a twenty-one-year-old beauty school student named

Veronica Hilliard, lived at the back of the storage facility in a trailer. The new silent alarm system had been going off randomly of late for no discernible reason, and she was tired of it. She came into the office and had the fatal misfortune of catching Harrison Lynch with a stethoscope held against the side of the company safe. Harrison had also apparently stolen himself a new knife somewhere along the way.

Cueball heard the screams and was out and running before he could begin to think about it. He climbed the chain link fence in nothing flat. He had his Smith & Wesson .357 in his hand before he crashed through the glass door of the storage office and got the drop on Harrison Lynch. The screamer was there with him, but she had stopped screaming—and everything else. Harrison was covered with blood. Cueball had about two pounds of pressure on his trigger with Harrison Lynch's forehead resting comfortable in his night-glow sights. Instead, he eased off the trigger and reached for his cuffs.

The famous Henry Wade personally prosecuted the case. With Cueball's testimony and photographs of the deceased, it took a Dallas County jury exactly seven minutes to decide that Harrison Lynch desperately needed to die in the state's electric chair for the murder of Veronica Hilliard. For good measure they tacked on forty years for breaking and entering. A month later, a Harris County jury took approximately eleven minutes longer to give him a second death sentence for the Curtis Gray murder. Three hours after the judge's gavel fell in Houston, Harrison Lynch found himself wrapped in chains and bound for Huntsville.

Sis years later, through efforts of a clique of bleeding-heart lawyers who were appealing his case on a number of frivolous grounds, Harrison still roosted on death row, eating all that good jailhouse food and waiting for his turn to ride the lightening. Then the Supreme Court abolished capital punishment. Harrison was transferred up to one of the regular maximum security units, this one on the Brazos River Bottom, where he was shocked to learn that a good portion of the inmates were stone cold psychopaths like himself. Thus he began his long sojourn with the Texas Department of Corrections. He spent his days chopping cotton and his nights trying to survive the various assaults that came his way from the muscle-bound homosexuals and Dixie Mafia types. Both groups viewed the killing of a harmless grandfather and the brutal murder of a pretty young woman as the moral equivalent to child molestation. But such are the wages of sin in the great State of Texas.

• • •

"So you had a chance to punch his ticket?" Micah said.

Cueball nodded in the darkness. "Yeah. That Smith & Wesson's trigger was honed to four pounds let-off. I've wondered since then if he ever knew how close he was to Gloryland."

"Do you regret the way it shook down?"

"Not one bit. I've never killed anybody, and I'm glad of it. As far as Jack goes, I didn't kill him by letting Harrison Lynch live that evening. Lynch is the one who did it, and he did it by exercising his own free will. I had nothing to do with his choice."

"I know you believe that intellectually, but is that how you really feel?"

Cueball sipped his drink and then stared off into the dark nowhere for a few seconds before he spoke. Then he laughed a little and shook his head. "Ain't life a bitch sometimes?"

[12]

"Homer Underwood is dead," Cueball broke the news to Micah Lanscomb in person. Another dark morning, another rude awakening with Micah in his skivvies and Cueball on his front steps.

"Goddammit," Micah said. Cueball waited for Micah to invite him in, to say something past his initial curse, to break down and cry—anything except simply stand there looking at him.

"I know you liked the old son-of-a-bitch," Cueball said.

Lanscomb hung his head forward and shut his eyes tightly. Perhaps he was praying.

"Get dressed," Cueball said. "You were seen with him yesterday, and you're a sitting duck in this trailer. You're moving in with me until all this blows over."

• • •

Cueball drove his burnished maroon Lincoln while Micah rode shotgun.

"I thought we were going to your house?" Micah said.

"We are. Afterwards," Cueball replied.

Micah sighed deeply, crossed his long, hairy arms over his chest and watched the dim and shadowy world illuminated by the car's headlights.

Cueball turned northeast on Market Street away from The Strand and drove ten blocks before turning back to the northwest on 2nd Street.

"We taking the ferry?" Micah asked.

"Nope," Cueball said.

"I don't know if I want to see this," Micah said.

"Neither do I, but—"

"But it's better that we know what we're dealing with," Micah finished the thought for him. "Something else you need to think about, Cueball."

"What?"

"Your testimony put Lynch in the death house. I know there was that Houston conviction, but spree killers aren't the most reasonable people on earth, so…"

"I've already thought about it."

"And?"

"I'm armed to the teeth and on my toes."

"How about Myrna?"

"She's packing her bags. I'm sending her to stay with her sister in Tyler. Pete is going to drive her later this morning. She'll be safe there. Besides that, Micah, she's as good with a gun as you are. Probably better."

Second Street became Ferry Road after a few blocks. The northern tip of the island dwindled into the darkness behind them and the glassy strip of the Intercoastal Gulf Waterway reflected the harsh lights of industry on the mainland beyond. Cueball turned off to the north and followed the shoreline.

Three small marinas, side by side, marked the last of the island's access to the waterway and the Gulf. And there, bathed in light, were a phalanx of police cruisers, sheriff's vehicles, and the coroner's wagon.

Leland Morgan walked up to Cueball and Micah as they approached. The heady, rancid smell of shrimp and crab boats mingled with the chemical odors of industry. At the end of the dock was what was left of Homer Underwood.

"The crabs took part of him, but it's Old Homer," Morgan said.

"Same shirt," Micah said.

"How's that?" Morgan asked.

"I said, it's the same shirt he was wearing when I saw him yesterday. And another thing, Morgan. If you say one word out of place, I'm going to take your goddamned gun and beat the hell out of you with it."

"Alright," Cueball said. "That's enough. Micah was Homer's friend. Probably his only friend in this world. Show a little respect, okay?"

Morgan nodded. "I will, and you two need to be the ones cutting me a little slack this time. I didn't have to call you, but I did because I knew Homer and Lanscomb were buddies."

"Point taken," Micah said grudgingly. "And I do appreciate it."

Morgan stepped aside and allowed the two men to join the sheriff's deputies and the medical examiner.

"Let's have it," Cueball said to the coroner, an older fellow near retirement age with salt and pepper hair and in need of a good shave. But then, every man there was in need of one, if not a stiff drink as well.

"There's a hole in his head that looks like a bullet hole. Could be a .25 caliber," the coroner said.

"'I'll die this island,'" Micah said.

"What'd ya say?" the coroner asked.

"One of the last things he told me. He said there'd be no one to mourn him when he shuffled off. Homer was born this island, he lived it, and now he's died it."

"Are you saying this is a suicide?" Morgan piped in.

"No and hell no," Micah said. "No way. If Homer ever owned a gun he long ago sold it for whiskey. He didn't kill himself."

"Well, if you say so," the coroner stated. "The crabs didn't get inside his cranium and I don't see any exit wounds. Chances are the bullet is still in there. I'll alert Ballistics to expect one."

"Where did you say they found him?" Cueball asked.

"He was washed up on the jetty a few hundred yards out," Morgan said and motioned toward the darkness and the northern tip of the island, with the Gulf of Mexico beyond. "A fisherman found him and called it in. We brought him in by boat since that was easier than hauling his body overland."

"We, hell!" a voice piped in from the boat anchored to the jetty. "I'm the one who brought him in."

"I know that voice," Cueball said.

One of the deputies shined his flashlight upwards at a red and grizzled face looking down on them.

"Spence Landau," Micah said and shook his head. A shrimper turned lawman, Landau ran the Galveston County Sheriff's Department boat patrol.

"It's me, alright," the voice said. "Now get that damned light outta my eyes before I make you eat it. Out of the way, I'm coming down."

"Any idea how the body got out there, Spence?" Cueball asked.

The other man shook his head. "He could have either been killed somewhere else and thrown off the dock or a jetty or out of a boat. Or he could have been whacked on the jetty or in a boat and then dumped. The one thing I'm sure of is that he wasn't dumped in the surf and washed out to where he was spotted. There's not enough of an ebb tide here to do that with a body."

"What I want to know is, will anybody give a shit?" Micah asked.

"I do," Landau said quietly. "I liked Homer. We've hoisted a few together over the years. As I understand it, he was a hell of a reporter in his time."

"That's right," Cueball said. "He ran the *Galveston Daily News* when I was a kid. Then he took to the bottle."

"And this is how they sometimes end up," Morgan said.

"The bottle didn't kill him," Micah said through clenched teeth.

"I'd say you're right about that," Morgan grudgingly agreed. "Don't worry, Lanscomb. Old Homer will get the same consideration anyone else would get."

"Yeah, right," Micah said bitterly. "The same consideration he would get if his name was Moody?"

Morgan grit his teeth. "You know, Lanscomb, sometimes I really hate you."

"Get in line."

Cueball took his friend's arm and swung him around and said, "Let's go. There's nothing we can do here but get in over our heads."

• • •

On the way home Cueball said, "I think I need to make a few calls and find out who Harrison Lynch palled around with up there at the Dreyfus Unit. If he's like most cons—and I imagine he is—he'll have one friend who knew all his ins and outs."

"And?"

"And then we go talk to him, whoever he is."

[13]

"You let Micah help you on this one, C.C.," Myrna said. She fussed around the breakfast table, moving jelly jars and setting out the proper silverware. The coffee steamed in his nostrils and threatened to scald the tip of his nose. Micah had skipped the meal and gone back into one of the guest bedrooms to finish sleeping.

"Cueball?" she asked when he didn't respond.

Cueball grunted.

"Are you listening, Mr. Boland?" she said.

"Of course I'm listening."

"But are you *hearing* what I'm saying? Take Micah with you to that prison!"

"Since when have I ever heard you?" Cueball asked with a laugh. "I never heard my momma, why should I be hearing you?"

"That's only because your momma had better sense than to even try to get through to you. Which means she had better sense than *me*, apparently."

"You do have a point," Cueball said. And with that, the conversation was over.

"I've got some phone calls to make," he told her when breakfast was done.

"No need to tell me," she said. She put her arms around his chest and squeezed him to her while he patted her arms.

"Up there in Tyler you be sure to keep all the doors locked and your gun loaded and handy."

"How long have we been together?" Myrna asked him.

"If you're asking what we're doing for our anniversary next week, that's a state secret. Allow an old man his remaining dignity and let him surprise his little sugar-girl, will you?"

Myrna kissed his cheek. "Just so long as all this mess is wrapped up by the time my birthday rolls around," she said. "That's the best present you could give me."

Cueball tried to think of something to say that would sound snappish and quick, but Myrna was already releasing him.

The front door bell rang. The caller turned out to be Pete Gofford, Cueball's pool hall manager.

Pete was coal black, about five-ten, and built like a Mack truck, with a massively broad chest and long arms that bulged with muscle. Back in his youth, Pete had been a grifter and a scam artist who had accumulated a half dozen arrests on a nice little rap sheet that made him, at least in the eyes of the police, a desperate criminal waiting to happen. Then in the late 1950s, he'd managed to get in the wrong place at the wrong time. As a consequence, he found himself installed on Huntsville's death row for the murder of a prominent Houston real estate broker who was slaughtered in a household robbery that went sour. The night his date with the chair came around, he fought the guards all the way from the holding cell to the death chamber. It took a half dozen big men five extra minutes to get him quelled halfway into submission. They were just in the process of strapping him in when the phone from the governor's office rang.

It was a temporary reprieve—ten days, issued by the State Supreme Court justice who wanted time to consider some disturbing stories put forth by his diligent and grossly underpaid attorney. The next week the reprieve became permanent when the court decided that a deathbed confession and some hitherto uncovered evidence changed the whole complexion of the case. It took several more months for the legal system to go through its red tape and shake Pete loose from the pen, but shortly after his release he received a full pardon on the basis of innocence. The warden later said that if it hadn't been for those five extra minutes of struggle, Pete Gofford would have been bound for glory, innocent or not. All Pete himself ever said was, "I didn't do it, so I didn't see no reason to let them redneck peckerwoods fry my ass the easy way."

Even in his criminal days, Pete had never been involved in anything heavier than petty larceny and the occasional rigged poker game, but his experience with the death house convinced him to go arrow-straight. Like Cueball, he was a native of the Island. The two met a few times over the years when they were home for visits. Not long after Cueball opened the pool hall, he tracked Gofford down, driving a cab in Houston. He offered Pete a job as manager of his pool hall. It was a move Cueball never regretted. These days Pete was rigidly honest. He was also smart and resourceful and able to run the place without any supervision, which left his employer free to get away when he needed to.

"'Bout ready, Miz Boland?" Pete asked, following Myrna into the kitchen.

"In a few minutes. Would you like some breakfast?"

"I done et."

"Who's going to handle the joint for us while you're gone?" Cueball asked.

"Tommy Smart," Pete said.

Cueball grinned and nodded. Tommy was a fine young pool player who had been hanging around the place since he was a little kid. Trustworthy and able, he would no doubt be gone in a couple of years as the big city tournaments beckoned. "Tommy Smart is pretty smart," he said. "He'll do."

Myrna finally got everything packed and satisfied herself that her two aging urchins could survive for a few days without her. Once Cueball heard Pete's Oldsmobile back out of the driveway, he picked up the phone and started calling in a few of his markers.

[14]

Leland Morgan stepped out of the elevator and into the vestibule of the Galveston County Medical Examiner's Office.

"Good morning, Lieutenant Morgan," the desk sergeant said.

"Geez, Mike. Didn't think I'd see you down here in the morgue. Who busted your chops?"

Mike Stratham was a veteran cop from Houston. The guy was in his late fifties and getting close to retirement. Morgan usually never gave the man the time of day. Today, he made it a point to be especially nice.

"Nobody did. I like it down here. It's cool all the time, nobody complains about anything. I don't have to take any crap, you know?"

Morgan chuckled. "The clientele is quiet, huh?"

Stratham smiled. "Yep. Just the way I like it. And I get to work a crossword puzzle every now and then as well. Say, do you know a four-letter word for 'boilerplate'?"

"Try 'form.' Say, I've got to take some pictures of Underwood before they do the autopsy. The lighting was bad out there on the docks where we brought him up."

"Ah. You're lucky that it hasn't already happened. Dr. Pierson got some kind of emergency call and had to leave, or you would have lost your last chance for a picture. You can go on ahead, Lieutenant." Stratham pushed a clipboard toward Morgan.

"Oh. Do I have to sign in?"

The clipboard paused halfway across the counter. "Not if you bring me a cup of coffee."

Morgan smiled. "I'd do that anyway, Mike."

"Thanks. Ah, to hell with it. You'd be the only name on the board all week if you did. Nobody really cares. Not sure what happens to these forms once they're full anyway. Not that I've ever seen one complete."

"Thanks, Mike," Morgan said, and walked on past the desk. He turned before he entered the morgue. "And don't let me forget to bring you that cup."

"I won't," Stratham said and went back to his crossword puzzle.

• • •

Leland Morgan donned a pair of rubber gloves and stepped into the examination room. Underwood's body—or what was left of it—was laid out on the cold table.

He walked around the body and glanced toward the drawn curtains. He paused for a moment, listening, then pulled a pocketknife from his pants and opened it. Bending low to Underwood's head, he probed into the gaping wound where the bullet that had taken Underwood's life had entered. After a moment of fishing around, he felt the metallic connection of the knife with the lead bullet. He removed the knife, closed it and dropped it in his pocket. He turned around and began opening drawers behind him. After a moment he came up with a pair of long and narrow forceps. He went back into Underwood's head with them and came up with the bullet. Back inside the drawer he found a large square of gauze. He placed the bullet in the center of the white cloth, wiped the forceps clean with it and replaced them, then slid the bullet into his pocket.

Leland Morgan smiled.

He made his way out to the front desk, waved to Sergeant Stratham and acted as though he had things to do and places to be. He waited for Stratham to say something about the coffee he had wanted, but when he didn't, Morgan increased his pace.

[15]

A guard captain ushered Cueball and Micah into the office of Don Kellman, warden of the Dreyfus Unit. Kellman was big, beefy, and hard-looking as befit the warden of the state's most secure prison facility. He was cordial without being overly effusive and gave the impression of being a man who could get a lot done in a short time.

"I hope you didn't mind my greasing the skids a little before we came over here," Cueball said.

Kellman smiled and shook his head. At fifty years of age, he was a career employee of the Texas prison system and a seasoned bureaucrat who knew how the game was played from way back yonder in the back yonder. Which meant that he was well aware that the grease on the skids could also be used to cover his ass. And he said so. "I really couldn't have let you interview Lynch's cellmate without a request from someone like your friend the senator. But with that request covering me, I am more than happy to oblige you. In my opinion, Lynch should never have been paroled."

"Why was he?" Micah asked.

"Because since he came here, his record has been flawless. Somewhere along the way he saw the possibility of parole and began to behave. He claimed to be a reformed man, and his record backed him up. Even here in Texas, parole boards occasionally show a little mercy. Misplaced mercy, in this case. And I told them so."

"You did?"

He nodded. "But they were of a different mind because of media pressure. Do you remember that big flap in the papers last year charging the parole board with being nothing more than a rubber stamp for prison officials?"

Cueball and Micah both nodded.

"There was a considerable measure of truth in the charges. As I'm sure you both know, the board is nothing more than a crew of well-heeled Rotarians who threw money at the governor's campaign, along with a couple of retired cops who were thrown in for window dressing. But the criticism stung, and they started getting serious about being independent-minded, like the press suggested. The release of Harrison Lynch is one of the results."

"So you didn't think he was reformed?" Micah asked.

"Hell no. Psychopaths don't reform. People like him suffer from a lack of conscience. But some of them do learn that life is much easier for them if they quit fighting society."

"But not Harrison Lynch?" Cueball asked.

"Oh my God, no. But he's very smart, and he's spent the last twenty years gaming the system. I imagine it amused him since he didn't have anything better to do. That is apart from all that math bullshit he was doing."

"Math?" Cueball asked.

"That's right. The guy went through the entire prison library on the subject, then started asking for more advanced stuff. Our library did have a couple of calculus texts, but the stuff he asked for, I've never heard of. Oh, crap. I forgot all about that."

"What?"

"I had a federal agent asking about Lynch the other day. I had to tell him he'd been paroled. The fellow didn't seem too pleased about that."

"What's that got to do with math?"

"Just that this federal guy asked if Lynch had been doing anything odd before he left us, and I mentioned the math stuff. For a minute there, I thought the guy had hung up on me."

"Huh. That's interesting. What's Lynch's former cellmate like?" Cueball asked.

Kellman smiled and played around with his paperweight for a few seconds. "Of similar disposition but not nearly as intelligent. I had him brought in from work detail and placed in his cell not long after he and Lynch said their goodbyes. Then I dropped by for a chat..."

• • •

"So, Sheer, looks like you've lost your buddy," Kellman said.

Sheer looked up from where he sat on his bunk and said, "Yes, Warden. But I've gained peace of mind."

"How's that?"

Sheer smiled at him and said nothing. The man appeared a little too full of himself to suit the warden's taste.

"Maybe I should move one of those big sisters in here with you," Kellman said. "I'm beginning to think you could do with a little smoothing out."

Aside from solitary confinement, which had very definite federal rules the prison had to abide by, throwing one of the big homosexuals in with a straight man was the biggest stick a warden could legally wield.

"Well, you know best, Warden," Sheer said, smiling cooperatively.

"That I do. If I didn't know better, though, I would say that you're downright pleased with yourself."

Sheer gave the very slightest of shrugs. "Maybe."

"Alright," Kellman said, "if there's something you feel you need to tell me you better speak now. I've got work to get done."

"Warden, all I can say is that Satan is about to have a long fall from heaven."

"And pray tell, exactly what does that mean? In ten words or less."

Sheer ran a hand slowly up the concrete wall above him, as if his fingertips were probing for microscopic irregularities in the concrete.

"Oh. Nothing, Warden. Or at least nothing that you won't hear about soon enough."

• • •

"So you think he knew," Cueball said. "Sheer knew Lynch was planning something. Something big, maybe. Only I don't see how the killing of his stepbrother and a beach comber is quite so big as all that.

Kellman nodded. "No doubt he did know something. You can have as much time as you need with him in a monitored interview room. He will be well shackled and there can be no physical contact. Good luck."

[16]

Wiley Sheer was a murderer. The man was what correctional officials called a "natural lifer." He would not leave his home in the Texas Department of Criminal Justice until such time as his blood ceased its circulation and a licensed medical doctor was certain enough of that fact to so note it.

A piece entitled "Equal Opportunity Killer" about Sheer appeared in *Texas Monthly* in the fall of 1983. He was interviewed in prison by one the magazine's newest, wet-behind-the-ears columnists, who brought a camera with him to the interview and took some pictures of Sheer. Mostly they were grainy, sepia-toned photos taken from rather odd and disturbing angles, but the most chilling one was shot dead-on. It showed Sheer sitting at a table with his head in his hands, his eyes shining above a bizarre, mocking grin, while a smoldering cigarette suspended from his razor-thin lips *a la* Humphrey Bogart.

Cueball remembered that photo. He noted that there had been little change in the man over the intervening years. At age forty-seven, Sheer still looked clean, strong, and eager. He looked happy and healthy. He also looked crazier than a peach orchard boar. Above all, he looked like a man who had a secret, one that he wasn't planning to tell anyone anytime soon. Cueball Boland laughed inwardly. He had a notion that he could change that plan.

• • •

"Three consecutive life sentences, Wiley," Cueball said. "With two hundred years tacked on top of that. You will never get out."

Wiley Sheer smiled. He loved attention and he was enjoying himself. "Did you come all the way up here to tell me that?"

"No, but it might have been worth the trip just to rub it in."

Sheer's smile turned into a smirk. It was about all he could manage in way of response. "Rub away."

Boland shook his head. "I'd rather hear all you know about Harrison Lynch."

Sheer's smirk morphed back into a smile, but this time it was a knowing smile, a smile that was wise and ancient in the way only a con's smile can be. "Now, why don't that surprise me?" he asked. "Well, then, you need to be aware that in my world knowledge is trade goods. You want mine, you got to offer some of yours. So what can you offer me for what I might know? And who the hell are you anyway? A cop?"

"Not any more."

"What then?"

"These days I run a pool hall down in Galveston. I also have a mid-sized security company."

"And?"

Cueball silenced him by putting his finger to his lips and saying, "Shush. Let me introduce myself my own way, Wiley. As for what I do, I get by, but I'm sure as hell not a rich man. Nor am I an elected official. So how do you think I got in here today to see you?"

"Shit, man, how should I know something like that? Maybe you blew the warden."

Boland laughed happily. "Nope. A state senator named Dell Ross called Kellman and told him let me in to talk to you. I know you're familiar with Senator Ross since he chairs the senate committee charged with oversight of the prison system, and lifers always know crap like that. Got any idea why he called the warden for me?"

Sheer raised his eyebrows.

"Because when I was a cop in Dallas and he was a student at Southern Methodist University, I cut him some slack on what could have been a drunken driving bust if I'd wanted to push it. SMU is a rich school with a lot of rich kids, and you better believe he wasn't the only one I helped out over the years. Oh, I cut plenty of poor kids the same kind of slack too. And that turned out to be a good investment as well because some of them aren't so poor any more. Some of them are high-powered lawyers and executives. And a lot of them are involved in politics in one way or another. But they all remember me and like to show their appreciation on those rare occasions when I need a little help. Besides that, I was raised on Galveston Island and I know where all the bodies are buried there too. Do you understand what I'm saying?"

Sheer's eyes gleamed brightly and his grin was something one would expect to find on a hammerhead shark—eager, mean, greedy. "You're telling me you're really in a position to help me? That's what you mean?"

Boland nodded, a lazy smile on his face.

"Then let's hear your offer."

"Okay. Here it is. The Pakalote Unit."

"What?"

"It's a new unit the prison system is building out near El Paso, where the climate is terrible, if you didn't know. And they named it after the right man, a man named Luther Pakalote who was warden of the old all-black Retrieve Unit for thirty years. That's the one the inmates called 'The Burning Hell.' Pakalote himself was known as 'Big Devil,' and he lived up to the name. So you can see why I say they're naming this new unit after the right fellow. It's being patterned after the federal super-max at Florence, Colorado, and the guys who are designing it are working closely with the prison system's lawyers to make sure that it just barely slides in under the federal prison standards. The operative word there is 'barely.' It'll be finished in about six months, and the first inmates shipped out there will be the five hundred most incorrigible assholes in the whole Texas system."

"What's this got to do with me?"

Boland ignored the question. "Let me tell you what life will be like at the Pakalote Unit. Each day will consist of twenty-three hours in lockdown in a five-by-eight cell. The other hour will be spent bouncing a basketball around in a miniature gym under the watchful eye of a pair of tobacco-chewing peckerwoods from some place like Silsbee or Conroe. They'll each have a nightstick, an electric cattle prod, a gut-deep hatred for people like you, and a yen for excitement." Here Boland broke off and shrugged and gave Sheer a goofy grin. "And you know what they say about situations like that. Shit happens!"

"Awww, man—"

"There will be no social contact with the other inmates. No bragging, no telling of war stories, no strutting around and impressing the new fish. Just the minimal number of visitors the feds require them to allow, which amounts to something like one every two months. Restricted phone privileges. Mandated weekly cavity searches. And this will be seven days a week, fifty-two weeks a year, stretching all the way out to eternity. For entertainment, if you want to call it that, each cell will have a TV set in the wall behind unbreakable Plexiglas. Two channels will be available. The old movie channel and the evangelical channel. But there'll be plenty of old Perry Mason paperbacks and stuff like that to read."

"Why are you laying this shit on me?"

"Because unless you tell me what I want to know here today, this shit is your future."

"Huh?"

"Believe it, Wiley. This is a one-time offer and you don't have but one chance to climb on the train. If I leave here today unhappy, you may as well get started packing your stuff, because your ass is headed west. So here it comes. You answer all my questions to my satisfaction, and out of the goodness of my heart I won't have you sent out there. And that's the best deal you're ever going to get from me."

Sheer smirked again, but this one wasn't a smirk with a lot of horsepower behind it. "You're bullshitting me. You don't have that kind of stroke."

Cueball nodded sagely. "I suppose a man could make that argument. But you might consider that it only took me fifteen minutes to arrange a visit with a triple lifer who was locked away in administrative segregation in a maximum-security unit. So do you want to risk it?"

"You're not offering anything of a positive nature," Sheer complained, his voice slipping easily into a plaintive whine.

"That's right, Wiley. I'm all stick and no carrot. But when you get back in the general population, you can ask any of the longtimers from Dallas about Cueball Boland. They'll tell you that making me happy was one of the wisest moves you ever made."

Sheer pondered this for a few moments, then shrugged. "Well, since I have nothing to gain by holding my mud, I guess I'll make you happy. Besides, I don't owe Harrison Lynch anything anyway."

"Smart move, Wiley my boy," Micah said.

"So what do you want to know?" Sheer asked.

"Gimme all you got," Cueball said. "Start wherever you want and set your own pace. Just don't leave anything out or you'll be headed west before you can fart."

Wiley Sheer stretched as well as he could in handcuffs and a waist chain. Then he wiggled around in his chair before looking across the table to meet Cueball's eyes. "Well, he claimed he had some old scores to settle. His family was rich folks."

"I don't think so," Micah said. "His father was a Pense. We're not even sure where the name 'Lynch' comes into it, but there's no rich islanders with that name." Micah turned to Cueball. "Were the Pense's rich?"

"At one time, maybe. If they were rich now, Jack wouldn't have been working for me."

"No," Sheer chimed in. "You don't understand. I'm talking about his *real* family. They're on top of the heap, but when he gets done with them, they'll be under the heap. That's all I know about it."

"His real family, you say," Cueball said. "Who are they?"

"That's the one thing I don't know because Harrison would never talk about it, no matter how I tried to pull it out of him. But I saw Harrison's commissary slip once. I didn't know you could have a commissary acount that big."

"How big?" Micah asked, before Cueball could.

"It was fifty thousand smackers. That's even against the rules."

Cueball chuckled. "There's only one rule, really, Wiley. The golden rule. You know what that is, right?"

"Yeah. Him who's got the gold, rules."

• • •

Thirty minutes later Micah and Cueball were on their way back home. "They must be keeping that new Pakalote Unit under wraps," Micah said. "I never miss reading the Houston paper or watching the news, and I haven't seen or heard a thing about it."

"You haven't?" Cueball asked.

"Nope."

"Well, don't feel too bad about that. Neither have I."

[17]

As soon as Micah and Cueball returned to town from Huntsville, Micah did his rounds, checking the various locations where NiteWise had security contracts.

When Micah finished his rounds, he pulled in at a doughnut place down on the Seawall for a cup of coffee. He had the bad fortune to run into Morgan, who had stopped only because he saw Boland's security company pickup parked outside the building.

"Out," Morgan said.

"Out of what?" Lanscomb countered.

That was another thing Morgan hated about the man—his obtuseness. He misinterpreted *everything*.

"Outside," Morgan said, nodding at the door. "We need to talk outside."

"Well, if you meant outside, why didn't you say outside?" Lanscomb asked. "I mean, the word 'out' has all sorts of existential possibilities not found in the word 'outside' due to the latter's geographic specificity."

Morgan ground his teeth and peered at the other man for a few seconds, trying to decide if he was serious or if he was being a smartass. He decided he was serious, which was all the worse in Morgan's view. Smart-ass he could handle. But a guy who would stand around in a Galveston coffee shop at 11:00 P.M. babbling about crap like "geographic specificity" had to be crazy. And literal-minded man that he was, Morgan always had trouble with crazy, especially when it came in packages like Micah Lanscomb.

Before Morgan could say anything else, Lanscomb gave him a bobbing nod and went through the door with one of his abrupt, plunging motions that set the cop's teeth on edge. Outside the doughnut shop, Morgan grabbed the other man's arm and whirled him around.

"What is your problem?" Micah asked, pulling loose from the angry cop.

"I'm sick of stubbing my toes on your heels in this investigation."

"So get ahead of things."

Morgan seethed. "Do you want to spend the rest of the night in jail?"

"For what?"

"We're out here all alone, so I guess it could be for anything I dream up."

Lanscomb sighed and shook his head. "Look, you're a badass cop. I give you that. I even respect it a little. But I'm Cueball Boland's man, and he's wired in tight with the people that matter here in Galveston. Old Island shit and all that. You know how these folks are. You and I are both outsiders, and we always will be. But like I said, I'm Cueball's guy and you ain't really anybody's guy. So if you lock me up for nothing you'll be pushing him a little too far. He'll go to his friends, after which the wrath of God will fall on your head and then you'll have to spend the next two weeks making excuses and explaining yourself. Tedious. Nobody profits. So why don't we cut all the Raymond Chandler cop versus P.I. bullshit and cooperate a little on this? I know you don't like Cueball. You may not even like me, charming fellow though I am. But what the hell? We both want the same thing."

"Which is finding out who killed Jack Pense," Morgan finally said. "I guess I can see that. Since he was your employee, you feel like you have a vested interest in the matter."

"Oh, it seems to go deeper than who killed Pense. A whole lot deeper, in fact. You see, we already know who did that. Or at least we're pretty sure we do."

"No shit? Who?"

"A guy named Harrison Lynch. Ever heard of him?"

"You're crazy. Lynch is in the joint doing life."

"Not any more, he isn't. The parole board got all misty-eyed and sprung him about three days ago."

Morgan regarded Micah with skepticism. "Okay, let's say that's true. But that doesn't mean he killed Pense."

"He's Pense's half-brother."

"How in hell did you find that out?"

"Old Island shit, I tell you. Cueball knew all along. They were all raised here in Galveston."

"But that still doesn't mean—"

"Lynch's cellmate said he told him he had some scores to settle with his family."

"You talked to his cellmate?" Morgan's voice was rising. He was both astounded and mad. "When?"

"Early this afternoon."

"Why didn't you let me know about this?"

"We tried. Cueball phoned the station as soon as we got back in town, but you weren't available."

"He should have tried harder to find me. This is withholding information," Morgan said between gritted teeth. "Maybe even obstructing justice. He's required to—"

"He's not required to do shit. That special Ranger commission, remember? Technically speaking, he's state and you're local. He can withhold anything he wants to withhold."

Morgan was poised somewhere between whipping out his pistol and killing this goofball or just admitting defeat. As it so often does, bureaucratic prudence overrode knightly valor: he dropped his shoulders and nodded in defeat. The goofball might be right. In fact he *was* right, but Leland Morgan didn't like it one damn bit.

"Besides, Cueball left a message for you to either call or come by the house. Didn't you get it?"

Morgan shook his head ruefully.

"Sorry about that," Micah said. "But where do we go from here? What do you want to do? Spend the rest of the evening booking me in and bringing a shit storm down your head, or would you rather invest the same time in getting a bulletin out on Lynch?"

[18]

The town lay inland half a dozen miles from the waters of the Gulf. On a breezy day the air had a salt tang to it and flocks of screeching gulls rode the zephyrs overhead, an ever-present reminder of the towns proximity to the waters that fostered it and gave it its life blood no less so than the growl and exhaust of the big trucks plying the highways between Texas City—the town's nearest neighbor and sister city—and Houston, thirty miles to the northwest. It was a working town and a tough town, if not a dingy town. And it was the perfect town for an itinerant blue-collar worker, his small-waisted and demure wife and his two towheaded children, ages five and seven.

His name was Bartholomew Elrood Dumas, but his co-workers called him Big Bart. His gut protruded a full twelve inches beyond his straining belt. His face, neck and hands were as red as a West Texas Indian—an Apache, perhaps, if such still walked the Earth. Big Bart was known to drink too much on a Friday night, go home and collapse on the couch and sleep half through Saturday. It was his only vice, and his wife Lorraine had come to expect it. She made sure the children didn't stick celery up his nose or put shaving cream in his hands and tickle his neck with a weed from the yard until he slapped himself, creating a spectacle far more entertaining than the Saturday-morning radio shows which invariably invaded his strange dreams as he slept the day away, snoring loud enough that the neighbors could hear all the while.

This Saturday in September, Big Bart Dumas was awakened by Lyle Fisher, his foreman from the Fleischman Oil Refinery on the Houston Ship Channel.

"Wha— wha—"

"Bart! Wake up!"

"Lyle? What the hell? Ain't it Sat—"

"It *is* Saturday," his roughneck foreman stated. "But I need your help, Bart."

"Where's Lorraine? Lorraine!"

A clatter of dishes reached his ears from the kitchen in their small, two-bedroom shotgun house.

"I got your missus' permission to wake you, Bart. Come on. There ain't much time."

• • •

"Where're you stayin' now, Lyle?" Big Bart asked as he rode alongside his foreman in his panel truck. "I mean, since you and the missus has split up?"

"Oh," Lyle said, "here and there. That's not important right now." Lyle Fisher turned his truck onto the highway headed east towards Galveston Island and Bart looked a question at him. "I'll tell you all about it as we go," Lyle said. "It's the reason I didn't tell you back at the house. You're not going to like doing this one damned bit, but it's got to be done."

"What's got to be done?" Bart asked, and then for good measure added: "You know that I trust you, boss."

"I wouldn't," Lyle said. "At least, not after today."

And then Lyle laid out the job for him as the truck bounced over potholes and on into the noonday sun.

• • •

The job was a kidnapping, to occur in broad daylight. Apparently a young girl of school age had gone and gotten herself in a family way. But the girl's father had money and was well-respected in society. The scandal alone would cost him a great deal of business. So the family had kept it quiet. They'd kept the girl home from school to have the baby and gave an obscure illness as the official reason. But the girl's father had no intention of raising a bastard child under his roof. And so the arrangements had all been made. Lyle was to kidnap the child while the grandfather was out of town on business and take him to a pre-arranged home.

"What about the kid's momma?" Bart asked. "She won't like it."

"No, I suspect she won't," Lyle said. "But it's better this way. It's better for the old man and the family, it's better for the girl, who is just a kid herself. And it's better for the baby."

When Lyle was finished laying it all out, along with as much of the back story that he dared to share, Bart caved in.

"Alright," he said. "I'll do it."

"There's a thousand dollars in it for you." Lyle handed Bart an envelope.

Big Bart looked down at the white linen envelope in his beefy, unwashed hands.

"Lyle, I don't—"

"Yes you do, and you will take it. That's an order. I know taking the kid is the right thing to do—the way it was explained to me and the way I've given it to you. So if it's right then there's no call to turn the money down, which is what you were about to do."

"Boss…I…"

Lyle turned to see a tear slip down the big man's cheek.

"Forget about it. Tell you what. I'll hold on to the envelope for you until the job is done. Then, when all's well, I'll give it back to you. You might lose it or something."

"Oh, shoot. You're right," Bart said. "Thanks, boss." He handed the envelope to Lyle, who folded it over and stuck it in his shirt pocket.

"Bart, this will be either the easiest or the hardest thing you've ever done. I don't see much of in-between anywhere in all this."

"Yes sir," Bart said, and said no more until they were driving up the ramp from the ferry onto the Island.

• Galveston, Texas

OCTOBER 1987

[19]

The alert for Harrison Lynch went out all over the county and state. Morgan met with Boland for coffee at Nell's the next morning where Boland gave him a rundown on what they'd learned the day before from Wiley Sheer.

"Family," Morgan said musingly. "Lynch told him that he had some bones to pick with his family."

"Right."

"What family does he have?"

"Well, we knew Jack was his stepbrother. His parents are dead, so what does that leave? Some cousins? Aunts and uncles? What?"

"That's what I guess I better find out," Morgan said.

"Then there was Underwood, who may have been killed because he knew something out of Harrison Lynch's past."

"You think he killed Homer Underwood?" Morgan asked.

"I think it's highly possible. The only thing that keeps me from giving you an unqualified 'yes' is the way old Homer lived. Right on the edge. As you know yourself, for old winos every day is sort of a minor miracle."

"We shouldn't have any problem finding him," Morgan said. "This is a small city and he can't have many resources after being locked up for twenty years.

"Don't count on it," Cueball said.

"How so?"

"For one thing, I learned from the warden up at the Dreyfus unit that Lynch is one hell of a lot smarter than anybody ever gave him credit for. Know what his I.Q. is by any chance?"

Morgan shook his head.

"One fifty-six. That puts him in the genius category. Plus he's been reading and plotting and planning for a long time. As far as resources go, we don't really know what he's got."

"So you're saying what, exactly?"

"Did you know I'm the cop who caught him in the first place up in Dallas?"

Morgan shook his head and looked at Boland with a new respect.

"I sure as hell was," Cueball said, and gave the other man a quick thumbnail version of the night Veronica Hilliard was murdered.

"Then you think he might come after you?" Morgan asked.

"Who knows? I'm trying to be ready if he does. But my point is that twenty years ago, I had him pegged as a low-wattage thrill killer and nothing more. Once he was on death row, he was out of sight and out of mind so I never gave him any more thought."

"Then he's obviously had this planned for a long time," Morgan said. "Just hit town and started killing."

Cueball nodded. "That's my analysis too."

Just then Micah came through the doors of the coffee shop and took a seat at their booth.

"What's on the burner, buddy?" Cueball asked.

"Weird shit, man. I just went down to the funeral home to see what would be involved in my arranging a decent funeral for old Homer. But your buddy Billy told me it had already been taken care of."

"Really?" Cueball asked. "By whom?"

"Blake & Purcell."

"You've got to be joking," Morgan said.

Blake & Purcell was an old-line law firm that had been on the Island forever. It drew the bulk of its business from a half dozen of the town's most prominent families. Blake & Purcell was all walnut paneling and brass-studded leather furniture. It trafficked in deeds, wills and trusts—a quiet sort of law that rarely saw the inside of a courtroom, not the kind of law one imagined arranging funerals for wino beachcombers.

"Then what—" Cueball began.

"That's all I know," Micah replied. "You know, the county can only release a body to the next of kin."

"Yeah, that's right."

"I plan to go down to the courthouse later this morning and see if I can find out what happened."

• • •

Three hours later Micah phoned Cueball at home. "It was a simple court order," he said. "Purcell asked for it. Judge Colvin granted it. There is no explanation on any of the paperwork. Is that legal?"

Boland sighed. "Why not? Judges can do pretty much what they want to do in cases like this. Who's going to second guess them?"

• • •

Two funerals in two days. Jack Pense's service was at the funeral home chapel and it was hopelessly sad. About forty people showed up, which was a respectable crowd for an obscure man like Pense. Jennifer couldn't keep it together and was in tears the whole time. Lieutenant Morgan attended. Cueball knew he was acting on the lawman's belief that the murderer often attends his victim's last rites. He and Boland both examined the crowd closely but saw no one who resembled Harrison Lynch or appeared in the least suspicious.

The next day about a dozen people attended Homer Underwood's graveside service at the old City Cemetery. Cueball had two surprises that morning. The first was when the presiding minister turned out to be Father Lloyd Wilkes, assistant rector of St. James Episcopal Church. The second surprise was the imposing woman who stood a little to one side, half hidden by a huge water oak. She wore dark glasses and a scarlet scarf.

As soon as the brief service was over, Cueball stepped around the tree to greet her.

"Hello, Vivian," he said.

"Hi, Charles." She was one of the few of his acquaintances who used his real name. She was also, he reflected, probably one of the few who even remembered it. She removed her sunglasses.

"Strange place for you to show up."

The woman smiled and said nothing. When she spoke, her eyes were half-lidded and full of amusement. "Charles, do you remember last year when I ran into you and that eccentric friend of yours...What's his name?"

"Micah."

"That's it. I ran into the two of you at Gaido's, and my friend called to say she couldn't make it as planned. So the three of us wound up having lunch together. Do you remember that day?"

He smiled and nodded.

"Then you should also remember that you and I got to talking about the people we had grown up with here in town and about their parents and their grandparents and all their quirks and foibles and about who shot whom for sleeping with which wife or husband...Do you recall that as well?"

"I do."

"And your friend got very exasperated at being left out of the conversation and finally made a pronouncement about the nature of the reverie we were having. What did he call it?"

Cueball laughed. "Old Island shit."

"Exactly. So just put my presence here today down as 'Old Island shit.'"

"Yeah?" Cueball said. "You must have known Homer from the old days."

"Everyone knew Homer. I'm surprised there aren't several hundred people here. He was once a very big man on this island."

"A reporter. That's what Micah tells me. I don't remember him well, though. I never had many dealings with the local paper until I came back from Dallas. I would, though, like to find out who killed him."

She nodded. "I know you would, and I'm not insensitive to your aims." Here she kissed the tip of her index finger and gently touched it to his nose. "Come by the house for coffee in a few days. Maybe we can help each other." Vivian turned as if to go.

Cueball became aware that his ears were red. There was something downright seductive about the woman and always had been. Supposedly it was once Vivian's sister, Lindy, who was the wild one in the family. It was Vivian, however, who had always had an affect on Cueball.

"Why not today?" he asked.

"Give it a week, Charles." With that she turned and walked away on high heels, dark-stockinged legs moving as if she were still in her prime.

Micah and Lieutenant Morgan materialized beside him.

"I think that now we know who paid for the funeral and arranged for the minister," Cueball said, nodding toward the woman. "We just don't know why."

"I'd say that's *her* business," Morgan stated.

Cueball turned to stare at the man. "Sure it is. But it means something."

"Probably it means she knew him from the old days and felt sorry for his ne'er-do-well ass."

Cueball frowned at the policeman. "All of Vivian DeMour's friends are old friends. That woman keeps her own counsel. If she wants to pay for Underwood's funeral, that's fine by me. Aside from that, she's one of my biggest clients, although I see her no more than once every couple of years. So don't read too much into anything I say, all right?"

"But?" Morgan asked.

"It's just…it seems to me she's been a little reclusive the last few years, which is why I was surprised to see her here."

"Okay, so she's a recluse." Morgan said.

"He didn't say *she's* a recluse," Micah countered. "He said she's been *a little reclusive*. All the difference in the world."

Morgan was seething once again. "God, but sometimes I wish I'd never left Lubbock!"

· · ·

Cueball walked up beside Father Lloyd Wilkes. "Fancy meeting you here," he said.

Father Lloyd Wilkes was a thin, witty man in his late thirties—a fair pool player who stopped by the pool hall a couple times a month to have a beer or two and lose a few games of eight ball to the joint's proprietor.

"Duty called, C.C. This is what I do. Along with weddings and christenings."

"Yeah, but for your parishioners. Not for the world at large."

The priest smiled. "I have never refused a request to conduct a funeral, not even for the unchurched. But according to the baptismal registry and parish records, Homer Underwood was born into, baptized into, and took his first communion at St. James."

"Really? That surprises me."

"Why? I've found that most derelicts have conventional backgrounds. Many have loving but disappointed families. Didn't Jesus himself speak to such people?"

"Point taken. But that brings to mind the question of why you were rooting through a seventy-year-old baptismal registry? Do you do that every time some wino dies here in town?"

"Let's say I had good guidance in that direction."

"I don't suppose you'd be willing to name your guide, would you?"

Wilkes laughed and slipped his prayer book into his pocket. "Dream on, C.C. A good Catholic boy like you should know about the sanctity of the confessional."

"A lapsed Catholic, Padre. I'm not much of a churchman."

"Come to St. James some Sunday morning and we'll fix that."

Cueball smiled and shook hands with the priest.

The day had grown warm. The sun was high overhead, and although the Gulf with its incessant tides, crashing waves and crying seagulls seemed a world removed from the verdant green of the cemetery, the smell of the sea abided.

• *Galveston, Texas*

NOVEMBER 1943

[20]

The knock on Longnight's door came as he was dressing to step out for lunch. He'd made up his mind to convince the chef of the hotel café to prepare him an egg sandwich made just the way he liked it. The knock at the door was to change all that—and to change Longnight's future as well.

"Just a minute," he called out, pulling his pants up over his starched white shirt, and slipping his belt on. He glanced about the room to make sure there was nothing that shouldn't be there and opened the door.

A thin, waspishly-dressed man of perhaps thirty-five greeted him. He wore a finely-tailored black suit and silk tie, yet looked out of place in it, as if he would rather have been at a bar or a boxing match somewhere.

"Sir. I have the honor of extending to you an invitation to take lunch with Mr. Salvatore Maceo on his balcony in exactly ten minutes."

"The answer is yes, of course," Longnight said.

"Very good sir. I will wait and escort you."

"I'll be ready to go in just a minute."

• • •

The Spanish-style furnishings of the Hotel Galvez ended inside the doorway to Salvatore Maceo's seventh-floor suite. As at the Maceo brothers' club, the suite was furnished in a South Pacific island motif. A set of bronze dolphins four feet from end to end emerged from bronze waves on the center of a large table in the entryway. An exact scale-model replica of Captain Cook's ship *Endeavor* stood out on a pedestal in the corner. The floor underneath was tiled in black volcanic granite.

The valet led Longnight through the suite and on past a set of French provincial doors to a spacious rooftop balcony. A man Longnight recognized from the Balinese Room sat at a large, round table beneath an unfurled umbrella. The man wore Bermuda shorts and a loose-fitting shirt with a garish floral print of reds, whites and yellows. On his feet he wore soft leather sandals. His legs and arms were tanned a golden brown as if he spent a great deal of time in the sun. He appeared to be about fifty.

"Mr. Talos," Salvatore Maceo said. He rose to his feet. "Good of you to join me on the spur of the moment."

"It was good of you to offer, Mr. Maceo." Longnight shook the man's hand and took the offered chair.

"Call me Sam," Maceo said. "My family and all of my friends do."

"Sam, then. Call me Randall. I don't like 'Randy.' It sounds too pornographic."

Maceo laughed.

So far, so good, Longnight thought.

"Talos. What is that? Greek?" Maceo asked.

"You might say. Talos was the name of one of the Titans, cast in bronze by Hephaestos and given as a gift to Zeus's lover Europa."

"You are Greek then. I don't mean to offend you, but you don't look Greek to me," Maceo said.

"What Greek ever does?" Longnight said. Maceo smiled warmly. "What are we having, Sam?"

"Well, actually I don't ever eat breakfast so my lunch is normally breakfast fare. I've taken the liberty of ordering eggs, American bacon, coffee, grapes, toast and a cigar—although not necessarily in that order."

"That sounds perfect," Longnight said.

Longnight took in a sweeping view of the Gulf of Mexico.

"A man could get used to this," he said.

"Yes," Maceo said. "I certainly have. It beats Palermo, though it reminds me of the coast of Sicily. The sand here is different. I prefer the taste of the Gulf of Mexico in my nose and on my tongue. I don't know why."

"I felt like that when I arrived. It'll be difficult for me to leave." Longnight's eyes rested on a horizon of forever blue.

"Same here," Maceo said. "That is, if I ever do. I'll probably die here. Tell me, Randall—I've seen you in my club several times over the last few weeks. You must like it to keep coming back night after night."

"I do," Longnight said, and turned to look at Sam Maceo. There was a close look in the man's eye. He was weighing, judging. And he was definitely fishing for something specific. In that instant, Longnight knew what the next question would be. It would be the same implied question, asked differently and much more directly.

"I'd like to know," Maceo began, "what about the Balinese Room appeals to you? What is it about my club, specifically, that calls you back there? Are you looking for something? Or maybe, someone?"

Longnight thought no more than a minute and then realized it would be best that he spoke honestly, off the cuff, particularly to this man.

"I like the excitement of the place," he said. "I enjoy watching the people. The music is superb, and the conversation is free and loose and generally uninhibited. People can relax there and be wholly themselves. It is the only place that I have found where every object fits. The South Seas Room in particular. I could live out the rest of my life in that room and become a fixture there."

This seemed to satisfy Maceo greatly. The man sighed wistfully and turned his gaze toward the horizon where the sea met the sky.

"Well spoken," Sam Maceo said after a moment. "You've put the right words to a feeling I've had since the day my brother and I opened the place. I'm glad you approve. Ah, here's our food. Let's eat. I don't normally talk business over lunch, but I've got some pressing matters today. So if you don't mind…"

"No. By all means," Longnight said.

The valet set a plate before each man and then deftly deposited a large silver tray in the center of the table. Everything that Maceo had promised was there in abundance.

Each man began to fill his plate in earnest.

"Do you know Abraham DeMour?" Maceo asked.

"I can't say as I do."

"Abe DeMour is the best architect on this island," Sam said.

"An architect. What does he design?"

"Who cares? If he is an architect he should be able to design anything. An engineer is supposed to be able to construct a toilet or build a bridge."

"Agreed," Longnight said.

"I have a proposal for you, Randall. I would like for you to approach Mr. DeMour. I would like to get his help to draw up the plans for a building."

"A club?" Longnight asked.

Maceo's eyebrows shot up.

"Not just a club," he said. "*The* Club. Or rather, *the* Club and *the* Hotel. All together. But Mr. DeMour is what we call Old Island people. Myself and my brother, we are not Old Island people. And people like DeMour, while they have their uses, have a tendency to look down upon us."

Longnight thought for just a moment. Here is the part where he must measure his words carefully. He must make no reference to gangsters, organized crime, or the like.

"I take it," Longnight said, "that I am not to intimate a connection with yourself or your brother when I approach Mr. DeMour."

"My brother? My brother has nothing to do with this, or at least not just now. The new hotel and club are my idea. But yes, just like you say, I wouldn't mention anything he doesn't need to know."

Longnight used the food before him as an excuse to remain silent and let the man lay it all out for him.

"I'm not telling you what to do, I'm just saying what I would do. If it were me, I'd pass myself off as an investor in hotels. Maybe an independent. I'd let it be known that I enjoy building them, but that when I'm done I normally take my share and head off into the sunset. I'm willing to bet that DeMour would be interested in designing a hotel that would stand up to the Galvez. Every man wants to make his mark. But that's just what I would do."

Maceo acted as if he were passing off a simple anecdote of little consequence, but Longnight got the full gravity of it.

"I do love these grand hotels," Longnight said.

"It's settled then," Sam Maceo said.

"Fine," Longnight said.

Maceo hesitated a moment and there was a distinct absence of any superfluous motion. Longnight suspected that he was preparing well for his next statement as if it was a thing he was practiced in doing.

"For doing this job for me," Maceo said. "I will compensate you adequately."

Longnight grinned. "No you won't," he said.

"How's that?" Sam said, his sandwich poised in midair. He looked up at Longnight.

"I won't accept compensation. Let's instead consider this a favor for a friend."

Maceo put down the sandwich and leaned back in his chair. The hint of a smile spread across his lips.

"People don't do favors for me," Maceo said. "Not unless they expect something in return. And the kind of favors I do—well, let's just say that you don't strike me as the kind of fellow who would need my kind of favor."

"Let's not call it a favor then. Let's just say that I'll do this because it intrigues me, and because I am likely to enjoy it."

Maceo laughed. "Then I won't owe you."

"Well," Longnight said. "There is one thing."

"Thank you," Maceo said. "For a moment I was afraid that you were trying to change my outlook on human nature."

"It's just that I do enjoy the Balinese Room."

"Ahh. Okay, then. Consider it already arranged. You will be my guest of honor whenever you come in. I will introduce you to anyone I feel you should meet, and all of your drinks will be on the house from now on."

"Good. Now it's settled," Longnight said.

[21]

Longnight had his first close call when Tad Blessing, the bellhop, came in without knocking to deliver a bottle of Highland Scotch. The kid caught Longnight with his hands still bloody.

"Wow! Did you cut yourself, Mister?" Tad asked.

Longnight slammed the bathroom door on the kid's face and then quickly apologized for it through the closed door.

"Look, kid. You scared me a little and I wasn't expecting you. Yeah, I got a little cut on my hand, but I'm alright."

"You need a doctor or something?" the kid asked.

"There's a sawbuck on the bureau. Go and get me a small bandage and hand it to me when I ask for it, okay?"

"Uh. Yeah. Sure thing!" The kid left and five minutes later there was a tap at the door.

Longnight opened the door, reached out with one hand and took the gauze. After a moment he stepped out into the room, his left thumb and wrist wrapped up with the white dressing.

"Say, Tad. I have a job for you," he said.

"Sure. Anything, Mr. Talos."

"First, how well can I trust you?"

"Honestly?" the kid asked.

"Sure, honestly."

Blessing laughed. "You can't trust no one. That's the truth. But trust you can buy."

"That's what I thought," Longnight chuckled. He had a good thing going here and was determined to ride it out as long as possible. The Galveston nights, the salt sea breeze, the endless crashing of the waves on the beach below the seawall, the crowds along The Strand and that perpetual layer of smoke just overhead in the Balinese Room—each of these things intoxicated him.

"Tell me what you want and I'll get it for you."

"This one's easy. The big secret is, my name is not Randall Talos. My last name is Lynch, but you're never to use that name. I don't have any friends, except maybe you, Tad. My friends call me Longnight. I don't want you to use that name, though, unless you're in my company and we're alone. You got that?"

"Sure thing," Blessing said, waiting for the real request.

"Good. Just so we understand each other. The other thing is simple. I want you to keep your ears to the ground for anyone asking after someone who goes by my nickname, Longnight. If you hear it mentioned, even in passing, I want to know immediately."

"Somebody's looking for you, ain't they?" Blessing asked.

Longnight chuckled. "You could say that. I have to stay one step ahead of the divorce lawyers, is all."

"Oh. Oh! Yeah. Sure. That's easy. I hear your nickname from anybody else, I come let you know."

"That's fine. I'll pay you in advance for it. How does a hundred dollars sound?"

"It sounds like a month worth of pay, to me." The kid was suddenly in great spirits, the faux pas about the blood on his hands already seemingly forgotten.

"Now, Tad. You mentioned something about whores the other night. Where might I find some?"

[22]

"Where to, sir? Post Office Street?"

"Post Office Street?" Longnight mused aloud, letting the sound of the street name echo in and out of his own head.

The cabbie, likely the second or third generation removed from Ireland and mingled with other less than pure stock, said, "Post Office Street it is. Good thing, too, cause I want to catch Sheila before the night is over."

"Sheila?" Longnight asked.

"Yeah. You might call me a regular. Best girl around and from the best house too."

"And what house would that be, my good man?"

"Mattie Wickett's. Say, you've never been there, have you now?"

"I haven't. Ms. Wickett's it is then," Longnight said.

And then the stranger in Bobby Donnegal's cab said something odd under his breath. "It may be a long night for Longnight."

Later that phrase would stick with Bobby. It would bother him until he decided it was important enough to tell somebody. But by then—as such things often work out—too much time had passed.

Longnight knew the instant the cab turned onto Post Office Street. He didn't see a street sign nor did he receive confirmation from the driver by word or gesture. The cabbie was lost in an imagined future moment with his beloved Sheila. He was humming a Glen Miller tune. It was for Longnight instead a moment of reverential insight.

While he waited he tasted the cool, salty night air through his window. He smelled cigarette smoke and thought of that wonderful place called the Balinese out on its long, lonely and roofed-over pier. He listened for and heard distant drunken laughter somewhere along the street outside the cab window.

And then the girl came unbidden into his thoughts, the daughter of the old architect. She with the innocent smile and the perfect, nearly ripe fruit. *She*. The one he had been permitted by fortune and fate to pluck.

He'd spent an hour with her in her own bedroom on the family estate, had entered and left via the trellis outside her window right after he'd said good night to her father on the front porch. He'd shaken the man's hand, full knowing what he was about to do.

Later, standing across the street in blackness beneath the draping branches of a willow, he watched the second-story windows for the light in her room which he had known would be there. Her voluptuous upper torso, bared and silhouetted by the electric light of a small chandelier, beckoned to him. And when he'd reached her window, the girl had helped him inside with one finger pressed to her lips.

She was sixteen and he was thirty-eight. She gave herself to him and he took her, gladly, though the house was quiet and he had to be slow and gentle or else risk a discovery he could ill afford.

She cried out at the moment, but it was into his gentle but firm fingers. He had anticipated her time and made certain she did not betray them both.

Afterward they lay together until her breathing shallowed and evened and Longnight knew she was asleep.

When he left, making his slow but steady way back down the trellis, it was with the most profound regret. He wanted to kill her. To feel her hot blood on his hands. He could not, though. If nothing else, Longnight was canny. There was so much to do, and he must avoid getting caught.

They had arrived. Post Office Street, at the entrance to Mattie Wickett's house of delights.

With a twirl of his cane, Longnight made his way up the narrow walkway and toward fulfillment.

[23]

His name was Denny Muldoon and he was a man who lived in perpetual pain. The pain was like a nest of rats in his stomach, gnawing, gnawing away. When he ate he wanted to die, and when he puked after eating it was all blood mixed with the food. He'd been to innumerable doctors and they'd all told him the same thing. "You have severe peptic ulcers." That was what they invariably said. Not ulcer, the singular, but the plural, as if the one hole in his stomach had found a mate and produced offspring.

He'd tried Milk of Magnesia, he'd tried all-meat diets, no-meat diets, exercise, lifting weights, swimming, heating pads and clabbered milk. He tried a week of fasting, excessive sex, baths in artesian wells, hot springs, covering himself with sand at Virginia Beach like that Edgar Cayce guy said you could do to cure anything from the blues to frostbite. He'd tried everything but the one sure cure he knew would take care of it forever. Amen. That cure was secured to a leather shoulder holster under his left arm, and if he was ever admitted to a hospital and was in his right mind, he'd employ it before they took it away from him.

But just right now he had forgotten about his stomach. His stomach might as well have been on vacation in the South of France or searching for the source of the Nile or anywhere else other than where Denny Muldoon was. At the moment he was in the downstairs hall at Mattie Wickett's whorehouse on Post Office Street in Galveston-fucking-Texas, looking at the most horrendous sight he had ever seen in his entire thirty-nine years on God's green earth.

The blood had dried a dirty brownish black, what an artist might call 'burnt umber.' It was splattered over the walls, the tables, the chairs, the floor. There were even splatters of it on the ceilings, fourteen feet overhead. There were splotches of it under—*under!*—the throw rugs, as if whoever had committed this most heinous of crimes had lifted a corner of one of the rugs, then dipped his hand into one of the holes he had made in his victims, then dripped it on the bare hardwood floor beneath before dropping the rug back into place.

"Why am I not throwing up? Huh?" he asked his stomach. "Where are you when I need you to do what you do best?"

No reply. His stomach was *in absentia*.

Six people had died in this one house, all within the space of an hour. The killer had locked the door from the inside and had begun his grim harvest sometime after midnight two nights ago.

Denny had been in Waco at the time, submerging his aching middle in water so hot it almost scalded him. But he'd had the presence of mind to stretch the phone cord into the bathroom and prop the damn thing up on the toilet where he could get to it from his mother's old porcelain claw tub.

When the call came and Agent Michaels had given him the word straight from J. Edgar himself, the pain had vanished and had yet to return.

"Get down to Galveston, Denny. Right now."

"Why? I just got home. I've got a week of vacation and I mean to use it."

"You can take a vacation any time. This is straight from Hoover. There's been a wholesale slaughter down there."

"Where?"

"The locals will fill you in. Get yourself going. Right now."

"Who did it?"

"We don't know but we think we know, and if we're right, when you find him you can't kill him. No matter what."

"Who?" Denny asked over the long line to Washington.

"Longnight," Les Michaels said.

"Sweet Jesus," Denny said. The phone clicked and went dead. He replaced it carefully on the hook on his porcelain bathroom throne, looked down at his distended stomach which had mysteriously quieted itself and then at the half empty blue bottle of Milk of Magnesia on the side of the tub.

"Alright," Denny had said to the peeling paper walls. "I'm coming."

The trip to Houston took four hours and Galveston another hour after that. The sun was just coming up when he crossed the causeway and rolled onto the island. He smelled the salt air and the brackish scent blowing up from San Luis Pass. He listened to the silence of his stomach.

Life was good—or good enough.

A local constable was waiting for him on the island side of the ferry.

"You Muldoon?" the constable asked.

• • •

He stepped out the back door to Mattie Wickett's place. A man in khakis and a fine western hat regarded him from past the bottom back porch step.

"Everybody around here asks me if I'm Muldoon," Denny told the man. "So yes, before you ask, I'm Muldoon."

"Thought so," the man said, and stepped up onto the porch. "I'm Bonaparte Foley, Texas Rangers. I've come to fetch you over to the Medical Examiner's officer. They're about to start the autopsies." Foley was a granite-faced fellow in his mid-thirties.

"Fine," Muldoon said. "After seeing the inside of that whorehouse, I'd say I need to see the handiwork itself as opposed to the leavings."

"Suit yourself. You'll see enough, I expect. Have you eaten?"

"Are you kidding me? No."

"Good," Foley said. "You shouldn't until much later. Myself, I don't think I'll have anything at all for a few days."

• • •

There were six tables. Each bore a body under a drab, grayish drop-cloth.

Foley introduced Muldoon to the doctor, a fellow who looked to be in his mid-forties named Lester Street. Muldoon chuckled to himself—it would have been a good name for some thoroughfare on the other side of the tracks. Dr. Street's assistant was a girl of perhaps twelve.

"Who's the kid?" Muldoon asked and jerked a thumb at the girl.

"My daughter," Street said. "Don't worry about her. She's already seen more than you'll likely see in your entire life." Street turned to the girl. "Does seeing dead people bother you, Molly?"

"No, Daddy. Dead people can't hurt nobody."

Dr. Street turned back and raised an eyebrow to Muldoon and Foley.

"Fine then," Muldoon said.

"Let's get started," Dr. Street said.

Street pulled the first cloth back to reveal a big, very badly cut-up body.

"Turn the sound equipment on, Molly," Street said.

Molly reached over to a wheeled cart that bore a large AC Delco sound-scriber with a silver toggle-switch. The thing lit up slowly and began to hum. A recessed turntable began to rotate.

"Today is November 28, 1943. My name is Dr. Lester Street of the Galveston County Coroner's Office and I am performing the autopsies of the man and the women who were killed at Mattie Wickett's whore— boarding-house…"

Street's monotonous voice continued with the name of the first subject, Hector "Bevo" Martindale. It detailed the body's weight, measurements, temperature and pallor, after which Street began to describe Martindale's injuries. The monologue lasted several minutes. Muldoon and Foley resigned themselves to an incredibly long day.

Neither man got interested until Street, bending over the body, gasped, then swore softly, then peered more closely into the open cavity of Bevo Martindale's chest.

"Don't crawl down in there, Doc," Muldoon said. "We may have to send out a search party if you get lost."

"Shut up," Dr. Street said. Molly raised her forefinger to her lips and made a shushing sound beneath a disapproving frown.

After several minutes of intense quiet, Street stood up straight and turned slowly to the two men. He glanced over at Molly and drew his fingers across his throat, at which point Molly flipped the switch on the sounder-scriber, turning it off.

"This big fellow," Street said, "was killed slow. And whoever did it knew what…"

"What?" Foley asked.

"Knew what he was doing," Street said.

"What the hell does that mean?"

"I'm sorry," Street said. "This is a bit of a shock for me. The killer is a surgeon, and a brilliant one."

"Alright," Muldoon said. "So we've got a brilliant, murdering butcher on our hands."

"Wait a minute," Foley said. "Dr. Street, you know the identity of the son-of-a-bitch who killed all these people?"

"Yeah, I think I do," Dr. Street admitted. He stepped away from the examination table and over to a shelf of medical reference books. He thrummed his fingers along the spines until he found the one he was looking for and pulled it from the shelf.

"Surgeon is only one of his many talents," Dr. Street continued. "He's also one of the most intelligent men in all the sciences." He handed the book to Foley, who was closest.

Foley read the title aloud and then the author's name. He handed the book to Muldoon.

"Yes. I know who he is," Muldoon said. "Yeah. You could say we're in deep shit."

[24]

Bonaparte Foley sat with Muldoon at a rickety table in a tavern on The Strand. The autopsies had lasted until the sun was down over inland Texas.

Foley folded his hands together and pressed his forefingers to his lips, waiting.

Muldoon ordered a gin and tonic. Foley was going to order a coke, but the Federal agent insisted on something stronger. Foley, with a wave of his hand, acquiesced and ordered a shot of bourbon.

"Okay," Muldoon said. "I'll spill it."

Foley didn't so much as bat an eye.

"His nickname is Longnight. That's the only name you need to know right now, and that about describes him. Crazier than a shit-house rat, that one. I've seen the file, and it's a doozey."

Foley sat and listened.

"There's a little town over in Virginia. It's nothing much to speak of, but there's a government-run shrink shop there. It's in an old country manor that survived everything the Civil War, Reconstruction and even the Depression could throw at it. That's where they house the real nut cases—but only the interesting ones. You know the kind I'm talking about. The kind of people who can do calculus in their heads while they play tubas and shit. There's one lady there who speaks thirty languages fluently, but she can't tie her shoes. Half the time she forgets she needs to go to the john and messes up her clothes."

Their drinks came and Muldoon knocked his back and asked for another from the barkeeper, a tall, good-looking Irishman. Foley sipped his bourbon. Muldoon regarded the bartender with an odd smile. The fellow quickly moved away.

"Into this place one fine day comes the maddest hatter of them all. This guy knows things. He knows things the German scientists never dreamed of. A hundred years ahead of his time. Right this minute there's a team trying to make head or tails of some of the scribblings we lifted from his apartment in Ohio. I've seen them. I can't begin to tell you how or why, but they have to do with magnetic resonance in the ultra-high frequency range where, theoretically, you can make something disappear. Also, he left some notes on hyper-communication using gravity. Instantaneous communication anywhere in the universe, if you can believe it."

"Sounds like science fiction," Foley said.

"Oh. It *is* science fiction. The only problem is, most of what he's written down—at least the parts that our top eggheads can understand—makes perfect sense. So, the thinking is that the rest of it must..."

"Must make perfect sense as well," Foley finished for him.

"Exactly."

"Except that he's a cold-blooded murdering son of a bitch," Foley said.

"He is that," Muldoon said, and began on his second drink, this time only tossing down half of it.

"So where is he now?" Foley asked.

"That I don't know."

"Would you tell me if you did?" Foley inquired in slow, measured words.

"No," Muldoon said. "Not until I get your word you won't kill him if you find him first."

"What makes you think I'd kill him?"

"Please give me some credit. I know how the Rangers work in situations like this. You're not about to leave a guy like this to the tender mercies of some halfwit jury. Not even a Texas jury."

Foley sat silent for a long moment. He reached out his hand, lifted the remainder of his drink and tossed it off in one whack.

"What's in it for Texas?" Foley asked.

"America wins World War II," Muldoon said.

"I'm not sure I follow."

"There is a project going on—I can't even tell you it's name—where we are trying to make a bomb."

"We've been making bombs since the war began," Foley replied. "Who cares?"

"The world will care, once we're done, *if* we do ever get done. This is a different kind of bomb. You must keep this under your hat, Ranger Foley—what I'm about to tell you."

Foley gave Muldoon a blank look. "I'm not the kind of fellow to run off and blab our secrets to the nazis or the nips. Out with it."

Muldoon waited.

Foley sighed. He raised his right hand and spoke in a tired voice, "I solemnly swear not to divulge any secret to me entrusted which shall compromise the integrity of the United States, her defenses, or her allies. That good enough for you?"

"It'll have to do." Muldoon leaned forward and crossed his arms on the table in front of him.

Foley slowly leaned forward, but not too close to the man. It was clear that Muldoon wished to impart a secret, but Foley was struck by the intimate nature of Muldoon's gesture. He waited.

"This bomb…one bomb. It will wipe out an entire city."

[25]

He had to see her again. The days and nights had blurred together. He was no longer certain how many he had cut up in an attempt to silence the voice. It didn't matter. This time it was a voice without words calling him. It was her. She haunted him, if the living could be said to truly haunt, and he very nearly could not complete a thought for the intrusion of her face or her smell or her soft laugh or even her weak cry of pleasure.

She was no more than sixteen, but at the same time she was as grown as they come. She was young and yet ancient. She was timeless. Like the Delphic Oracle, she recognized the power in him. She knew his unstoppable nature. And she stood at the center of the storm that was Longnight. She was the warm waters that fed him and gave him strength.

This night, he walked from the Galvez down empty streets. He turned on Broadway Street as if by instinct and slowly paced the twelve blocks until he stood across the street from the DeMour house.

This night the house was dark. Not a single candle flame flickered behind the black windows of the dark three-story facade.

His black, double-breasted silk suit shushed as he stepped quick and cat-like across the wide street, his boots whispering quietly over the flat, even brick. He was Longnight. He was a force of nature. He was the soul of darkness.

• • •

Their first meeting had been a seven-course meal hosted by the girl's father. Longnight could barely recall the man's name. The man himself was unimportant—except, of course, in his own mind. All that Longnight could remember for certain was that the man was an architect who kept his offices in the Sealy Building down near The Strand. He was wealthy, he was singularly vapid and would look fine stuffed and mounted alongside the game trophies in his second-floor billiard lounge. That night before the meal, Longnight had played a round of billiards with the man, bested him twice—briskly—and then permitted the man to win by setting up the final ball for him while missing his own shot at the same time.

At dinner, the girl, along with the rest of the family, sat at the far end of the table beside her sister. The sister was stiff and cold to him. He had no interest in her.

Longnight sat next to the architect and opposite the architect's wife, a small woman with delicate features and a hollow color about her, as if she suffered from anemia. Possibly she had inhibitions against eating.

Despite the conversation, which was boring beyond belief, Longnight's full attention was on the girl, though he very carefully did not allow his gaze to rest upon her. In the briefest of moments when their eyes first locked as she came into the room, he knew all he needed to know. The pupils of her eyes swelled to take him in. She cast her gaze away from him, quickly, but that brief instant was all he needed. He knew she was for him. And she knew as well.

That first night, long after he said his goodbyes, Longnight had his first taste of real womanhood. And he savored every moment of it. He remembered the patterns in her face, the thrumming of her heart against his far greater weight. And he cherished her every whisper.

• • •

Tonight would be his final visit. He would soon quit the island. He would take his car to the ferry and then the mainland, would disappear into the dark beyond and whatever destination awaited him.

He climbed the trellis in shadow. Her window was open and he slipped inside.

"I've waited for you," she whispered. "I've waited every night."

"I know," he said softly. His eyes adjusted slowly to the gloom. She took his coat from him and placed it on the back of her bureau chair, then she came into his arms and kissed him.

"Ssh," she whispered. "My sister is in the next room."

He placed his hands against the small of her back and raised her up off the floor and into a full embrace.

"Love me tonight," she whispered into his ear as he pressed his lips into her neck.

• • •

Afterwards they lay together. Moonlight fell across the floor beside them and the music in his head was Debussy's *Clair de lune*. Fitting and proper, it was.

"I have a secret," she whispered ever-so-softly.

"Tell me."

"Not until I hear your darkest one," she said.

"Your price is too high," he said. "The lone secret of a sixteen year-old girl against my darkest secret. Tell me your secret, and I will choose one of mine. And I promise, it will be far darker than yours could ever be."

"Done," she said.

"So. Out with it."

She placed her lips against his ear. "I am going to be a mother," she said. "And you are the father."

At that moment the world seemed to shift on its axis. Now, no matter what happened, if what the girl said was true, there would be no stopping him. Not even if they killed him. His progeny would go on.

"You have outdone me," he said.

"Your secret," she said. "Tell me."

"Do you know of the murders on Post Office Street?"

"Yes. It is all anyone can talk about. Are you here to investigate it?"

"No. It was my work. I am the killer. I am the one they call Longnight. And now you know my darkest secret."

"Oh my God. Make love to me. Quickly. Before I scream."

"Hush," he said gently and smothered her mouth with his.

• • •

The next morning when she awoke Longnight was gone. She found his gift for her on the dresser. It was a leather book. She picked it up and pressed it to her nose, drawing in the strong, yet pleasing odors of the tannic acid from which it had been cured. The leaves were a creamy white and cleanly cut. She ruffled them and saw strange figures there. Some she recognized as mathematics symbols. Others appeared to be of an electrical nature, as if the author had merged the two sciences into one with a deft hand. The lettering was cursive and spidery, and there were little drawings here and there, interspersed through the text as if graphically demonstrating some idea before going on.

The daughter of Abraham DeMour sighed and her hand traced a slow circle around her bare naval.

"My baby," she whispered to herself. "My little Longnight."

The doorknob rattled and she started. She took three steps to the bed and slipped the book beneath the bed covers.

• *Galveston, Texas*

OCTOBER 1987

[26]

It was past noon, the day following Homer Underwood's funeral. The sun was bright overhead. Not a solitary cloud to mar the forever blue bowl of sky.

Micah Lanscomb would have given anything for a few days on any given ranch far enough away from the coast that you couldn't smell the ocean air—a few good long days with a horse and lots of pasture land to run it on. He'd not ridden a horse in over ten years, but he couldn't get the idea out of his head that if he were on horseback instead of at the wheel of a little Daihatsu pickup truck, he'd have time to think better, to work it all out better, and come upon something—or, for that matter, anything—that would send him off in the right direction towards the killer of Jack Pense and Homer Underwood. Or *killers*, if that was indeed the case. And he couldn't shake the notion that the two were somehow related. Not that there was much evidence pointing either way. It was just that a certain conversation which had occurred in front of a greasy spoon restaurant along the seawall hung with him.

Micah's mind kept going back to that doorway at the top of the stairs in the quiet, dark of the DeMour warehouse. It was Cueball's oldest account, this he knew. But what he knew about the DeMours he could have fit on the cover of a matchbook with a magic marker. There was a name rattling around in his head. If he thought long and hard enough on it, he might remember it. Isaac? Abraham? Something like that. But the guy was long dead and gone. He'd been an architect and the patriarch of the Old Island family. Old money. There were three DeMour warehouses, the oldest of which was the one on the island—the one where Jack Pense had breathed his last. But then there were the two newer ones on the ship channel. Most of the business went through there. From Cueball's stories, the dredging of the ship channel had meant the beginning of the end for Old Galveston. But the new warehouses, that was where the commerce came in. The DeMour offices were there. And—

"God Almighty," Micah swore under his breath. "We've been looking around for Old Island shit. What we need to be looking for is New Mainland shit."

Micah Lanscomb U-turned abruptly in the middle of Seawall Boulevard—what an old-timer such as Homer or Cueball might call a 'Barney Oldfield'—and made his way back to the intersection of Seawall with the I-45 Freeway leading to the mainland.

Possibly Cueball could wait a few days for a meeting with Vivian DeMour, which was what he appeared to be doing. And if such a meeting ever did occur—and the prospect seemed remote to Micha's own reckoning—the two of them would be more likely to end up doing nothing more than reminisce about the old days and the old ways over old high school yearbooks while they emptied one bottle of liquor after another until they passed out on each other's shoulders. In other words, immerse themselves head and shoulders in 'Old Island shit' and not get a damned thing done. But an old dog, now. An old dog such as himself? He had to do his own rooting around for his own bones. And such a dog couldn't be made to wait for the nod of his master before doing so.

Micah Lanscomb left the island, almost wishing he were on foot—or better yet, on horseback—and headed off into the blue horizon to God only knew where. But instead he got the little Japanese-made truck up to sixty along the long ride over the bridge to the mainland. Which was somehow just off-center of perfect.

• • •

Nestled against the southern end of Galveston Bay is a line of slips for the big ships: the oil tankers and supertankers that fed the ugly refineries, the equally large freighters with their boxcars laden with a variety of products from fingernail clippers to Toyota trucks. Across from the slips the warehouses began. Some of the big companies had their own internal security. Most of the time you never saw these guys at all. Cueball had explained it all to him once when Micah had offered to go after some of the larger accounts that appeared to be just begging for service. "You put a guy in a room with about thirty TV monitors and a VCR tape on constant record and you cycle those monitors through all the cameras you've got strung out over about fifty acres of space. You relieve him every eight or twelve hours and what you got is the world's least expensive security operation."

"That's for crap," Micah said. Cueball had agreed. He didn't run things that way. His guys moved around constantly, varied their pattern, and were aware of every door, every nook and cranny of every outfit they covered. Plus they wrote reports on the seemingly most innocuous things. Cueball himself read every goddamned report religiously. Cueball was notorious for showing up at any given hour of the day or night—checking things out and letting it be clearly known that there was someone minding the store. The Old Island people who owned some of the bigger warehouses liked it Cueball's way. As Cueball explained it, they liked the "personal touch." And Micah had agreed.

• • •

The docks were in full swing. Men walked about with a brisk stride. Front-end loaders moved in smooth but constant motion, carrying away the sheer tonnage of materiel unloaded from the ships by great cranes. The heavily-laden loaders swarmed to their respective warehouses and swarmed back, hungry for another load. And all the while the cacophony of sound carried its own rhythm, a raucous but steady pulse beat. Fifty, a hundred years ago, these same docks would have held longshoremen, stevedores and yelling bosses.

Micah parked his pickup alongside the company and employee vehicles to the side of the warehouse, went around the corner and walked into the cool shade of the building.

He didn't know any of the men and women he saw there. They worked with a bored and yet mindless familiarity with the various tools of their trade: forklift, broom handle and clipboard. Some looked at him as he passed, a guy in uniform yet not apparently a cop. Someone to disregard. Micah liked it better that way. He nodded at those few who very nearly dared to accost him. Something in his eyes and his taciturn manner convinced them otherwise. He stepped through a doorway with a logo that said "ASG" on it and into an air-conditioned office area. A dumpy-looking woman in her early to mid-sixties with too dark lipstick and blond curls done up by a hairdresser who lacked imagination sat at the counter.

"Excuse me," Micah said, and the lady turned.

"Yes?"

"Accounting. Please."

"Oh. Right. Through that door there and up the stairs."

"Much obliged," he said, already in motion.

"Any time, honey," the lady said. "You come see me any time."

"By the way," Micah said, pausing in mid-step. "What's ASG stand for?"

"You know, honey, I don't rightly know. But that's who pays the bills."

"And the paycheck?" he asked.

"Right. And the paycheck."

Micah passed through the door and down a long corridor lined with offices, most of them open and about half of them vacant except for the obligatory desk, papers, game and fish trophies and the like. Then a long staircase going straight up into darkness.

At the top of the stairs Micah saw a set of batwing doors, each with a round window. He pushed and entered.

• • •

"Help you?" a squeaky voice asked. Micah turned his head. The voice came from a short, elderly man with a broad forehead, silver hair, a hooked nose and a ruddy complexion. He stood up from a low table littered with what appeared to be invoices, a set of double-entry green on deep-green account ledgers, and an old nine-key punch calculator, the mechanical kind. He wiped his brow then placed his hands on his hips and tilted backwards slightly, as if to pop his back.

"I don't rightly know," Micah said. "All I know is I'll have hell to pay if we can't figure out who to make the check out to and where to send it."

"What check?"

"For the return of the commissary money."

"What the hell are you talking about?" the man asked.

"Oh," Micah said. "You see, when you send money to someone who is in prison these days, you have to do it to their commissary account through a wire system to the Department of Corrections."

"We don't do that here," the man said. "This is an import company. You're in the wrong place."

"Oh," Micah said. "Well, I'm pretty sure this is ASG, only nothing on the account ledger from the TDC says any of the money came from ASG, so there's my quandary."

"I don't get you," the man said and just stood there.

Micah wiped his own brow. "It gets hot up here, don't it?" he asked.

"It sure does."

"My name's Micah Lanscomb. I help C.C. Boland with the security on the Island."

"This ain't the Island," the man said.

"You got that right. Like I said, I'm Micah Lanscomb." Micah held out his hand and gave the man an expectant look. The man took his hand.

"Hulon Bailey," he said. "But most people call me Hub. I don't see how I can help you and I've got to handle all these invoices before quitting time." Hub Bailey traced a finger across an invoice as if looking for something, possibly an out of place decimal point.

"Well, since Harrison can't be found, the money has to go somewhere," Micah said. "Cueball told me to return it."

"Harrison?" Hub Bailey asked.

"That's right. Harrison Lynch."

Hub Bailey's eyes did a little number, as if he were running a mechanical calculation of his own back of his eyes. His eyelids jogged up and down for an instant, his brow furrowed slightly, and he rocked backwards a few inches.

"You alright?" Micah asked.

"Sure," Bailey said, suddenly bright and interested. Bailey wiped his lips with his sleeve needlessly. "Sure. Have a seat, uh..."

"Micah."

"Sure. Have a seat, Micah."

Micah sat across from the man in the little wooden chair. The moment he sat down he felt the hair raise on the nape of his neck and he said the first thing that popped into his head.

"I think maybe Vivian got it all wrong."

"What's that you say?" Hub Bailey asked. His eyebrows shot up.

"Nothing, really," Micah said, and made it a point to yawn. "It's just that what I'm about to say can't go beyond this room, alright?"

"Sure. Absolutely, Micah. We don't talk here, and the walls can't remember squat."

Micah paused a moment for drama. "Whenever it comes to matters of family and money, it's best to do what you're told and not ask any questions. The only problem is that sometimes you don't get enough information to carry out an order. I'm sure you're familiar with that sort of problem, being an accountant and all."

"Oh, yeah. Man, you sure said it! That's the whole crux of the problem since Methuselah was a pup!"

"Exactly," Micah said. "So you've got the DeMours and the Penses and you've got Lynch, only he's really a DeMour—but for God's sake I can't exactly say that out loud, now can I?" Micah didn't give Hub Bailey the chance to answer, but instead plunged onward. "So when Cueball says the fifty thousand has to be returned..."

"Fifty thousand?"

"Yeah. Fifty—"

"We never sent Harrison near that much. Unless—"

"Unless?" Micah asked.

There was a terrible, still moment when Micah was afraid that Hub Bailey would realize his error and call up the powers that be and have Micah escorted off or arrested or both, but then in the next instant that fear was transmuted to a species of satisfaction.

"*She* did it," Hub Bailey said. "I told her not to! I told her again and again you can't send that kind of money through the prison system. You just can't do it. I mean, administratively, they can't handle that kind of thing. It would raise too many eyebrows."

"Exactly," Micah said. "That's why this has to be done so quietly. It wasn't supposed to happen, but then again, who would ever know that the pardons and paroles folks would set him free. The money that came back was dropped off in cash at C.C.'s house by a friend of his from Austin. C.C. had to make deposits in less than ten thousand dollar increments so that it wouldn't raise any eyebrows at the federal level. You know, so that no questions would be raised *there* and the money be traced back to the prison system and people lose their jobs, if you know what I mean. And so now we've got to get it back where it belongs. And I guess that's where you come in."

Hub Bailey let his head flop back in his chair and stared up at the ceiling.

"Good God," he said. "I tried to tell Vivian. I tried to tell her. I thought if she wouldn't listen to me she might listen to Homer. And now he's dead."

"Homer?" Micah asked quietly.

"Yeah," Hub Bailey sighed. Micah himself breathed an inward sigh of relief. "She was sitting right where you are and asking me to push the funds through...like he would need that much in prison. Like he would ever, ever get out."

"But he is out," Micah said.

"Yeah. That's what I've heard."

"I think he came looking for the truth about his family. And he hasn't found it yet." It was the one truthful thing—Micah realized after—that he'd said during his entire visit.

[27]

The sun was beginning to dip low in the western sky when Cueball rang Vivian DeMour's doorbell. Vivian herself answered the door. From within came the heady scent of steeping cinnamon tea and the distant rattle of a large outdoor air-conditioner unit. It took quite a bit of power to keep a three-story mansion cool on the Texas coast in high summer, and the DeMour place was one of those mid-nineteenth century homes with fourteen foot ceilings and broad-paned, crenelated windows. But even in the late fall there were warm days, like this one.

"Charles," Vivian said. "I thought you were never coming."

"No chance of that, Viv, although I can't stay long. I think Myrna may be jealous of our friendship." Cueball gave her his best grin.

"Fiddlesticks to that," Vivian said. "I've known Myrna Hutchins all her life. If anybody's jealous, it should be me, even though I'm ten years senior to both of you. Now come on in here before I change my mind and send you back home." Vivian held the screen door open and Cueball stepped into the foyer.

"Myrna's last name is Boland now," Cueball said.

Vivian ignored the comment. "I've just made some tea," she said. "Want some?"

Cueball ran his hand through his hair, wiping away the last drying sweat of a long, hot day. "Iced tea sounds fine," he said. "Especially if it's laced with something."

"Maybe I'll spice it a bit. We could make a game of you trying to figure out what the secret ingredient is."

"I'll take it."

Cueball followed her into her living room, took the high-backed suede chair she gestured towards, and waited.

She was back within three minutes.

"Say," Cueball said, "this room hasn't changed a bit since I was a kid, has it?"

"No," she said, taking the end of the couch next to his chair and setting two mason jars of tea down on the coffee table in front of them. "This was my great-grandfather's place. After Daddy died...when was that? 1950. After Momma died, Daddy didn't have the heart to change a damned thing. And after he passed, well, it fell to me, and I couldn't change it either."

"Is the whole house like this?"

Vivian laughed. "No. Just the living room, the dining room and the library. The kitchen is all modern now. And my room is Momma's and Daddy's old room. I even have an art room up on the third floor. It was my room when I was a kid."

Cueball took a long quaff of his tea. "Tastes like a hint of absinthe," he said.

Vivian smiled. Cueball noted that she was holding herself a bit in reserve. She wasn't showing her poker hand. Yet.

"Say, Viv. There's a couple of things we need to talk about."

"Old Island shit, as your friend so charmingly put it?"

"Yeah."

"Fire away, C.C. I'm ready."

"I know you are, and that's what bothers me. Ever since I saw you at Homer Underwood's funeral, something's been itching the back of my mind."

"You want to know how I know Homer."

"Well, sure. But mostly I need to know about Harrison Lynch. And your sister."

"Lindy has been dead for twenty years, C.C. I'm alright talking about her and her mistakes."

"Well, that's fine then. I've never understood much about all that family business of yours. There was talk back in the day. I heard some of it way up in Dallas when I was a cop."

"You mean," she said, setting her glass of tea down carefully on its coaster, "you found out who you had really arrested before you had to testify at his trial. I've never held that against you, C.C."

"No, I didn't know then. I just put it together in the last few days."

She nodded. "Harrison was a killer. I think Lindy was hoping for an angel, and what she got was a demon instead."

"Well, would you mind telling me the story? And not the story that's been told outside your front door or to the neighbors, but the real one."

Vivian DeMour leaned back on the sofa, laced her hands together over her belly and sighed.

"I *would* mind, C.C.," she said.

"I know," he told her after a long, thoughtful moment. "But I think you need to. And not for me, but for you."

Vivian relaxed. She lifted her eyes up towards the ceiling where they came to rest on the isinglass chandelier.

"Lindy was the wild one," she began, and didn't stop until it was all said. "You know, she died before Harrison was convicted and sent to prison. When he was an infant in her arms, he was kidnapped by two men, and from right there about where you're sitting. They came in the house when Daddy was in Atlanta on business and Momma was staying in a sanitarium in Marlin getting three mineral baths a day and coughing her lungs up. It's not odd that Momma died before Daddy, being sick and all, but I always suspected that he was why she was sick in the first place.

"But I was talking about Lindy.

"Lindy's life was nothing but trouble. She was just sixteen. It was a scandal, let me tell you. Daddy took both of us kids out of school on the excuse that we were sick, just like Momma. Lindy was to have the baby here at home. I was to help her with taking care of it. That's how it was supposed to happen, and pretty much did, right up until the kidnapping. We were babies ourselves, Lindy and me. But Daddy kept the whole affair hush-hush as far as the community was concerned. I think it was the servants who talked and the rumor made the rounds of the Island. I'm still hearing it to this day.

"Who was the father? You don't want to know, C.C. That's the blackest secret of all. And whatever you may have heard, it's nothing compared to the truth. Just know that the father has been dead these many years. He was older than her by twenty years. That in itself would have been a scandal. But no. He was supposed to be a gentleman. Longnight was invited under my father's roof and at his first opportunity he took advantage of my sister and her wild ways. And the child? Harrison? This is the amazing part. Harrison lived his first eight years after the kidnapping right here on the Island, less than two miles from this house. Right under our very noses. I found that out later from Jack.

"Later in life Jacky found out who his little brother actually was. His mother confessed on her deathbed to keeping Harrison after her husband kidnapped him. There was money involved too. I suspected my own father of collusion in the kidnapping, but there has never been any evidence. Something went awry with the kidnapping, though, and the child didn't end up where he was supposed to—where the conspirators had planned. That much I know. That much of the story came out when Jack's mother died.

"Why do you think I asked you to hire Jack Pense all those years ago, C.C.? It was to keep what little family I have left—or maybe you could see it as extended family, even though we're not blood-related. I wanted somehow to help him. And Harrison...he never knew who he was...where he came from. And now he's in prison for the rest of his life."

"No, he's not, Vivian," Cueball said softly.

"What?"

"He's free. And he's killed again. It was your nephew who killed Jack. And he also killed old Homer."

"No!"

"Yes," Cueball said.

Vivian began sobbing. Cueball restrained himself from reaching out to her for a moment, then, being Cueball, he pulled a handkerchief from his shirt pocket and handed it to her.

"People don't carry handkerchiefs anymore, C.C.," she said and almost laughed between her sobs.

"I know," he said.

"You know, we held out hope that the baby would come back to us one day. Lindy thought he was an angel of God, only because it would take a fallen angel to sire such a beautiful thing. Only fallen angels can come down to Earth."

"A fallen angel?" Cueball asked.

"Harrison Lynch's father." Vivian said. "If you knew who I was talking about, you would agree that he was either a fallen angel or a demon straight from hell. I suppose it all works out the same. Daddy even named his import company after Lindy's label for the baby."

"Did he? Which company, Viv? You have so many."

"A.S.G. It stands for Angel Sent of God."

"The story sounds good, Viv." Cueball said. "Believable, even."

"But?"

"As long as I've known you, something about it doesn't compute. I'll leave it there if you want."

She nodded and made as if to stand. "Yes. Let's leave it there. No good can come of any of it. There is one thing I have to ask you, Charles, before you go."

"Go ahead."

"You're trying to track down Harrison. He *is* family. I won't have you killing him."

"No one said anything about killing him, Vivian. But he doesn't belong outside of prison bars. Surely you realize that?"

Vivian DeMour hesitated, then slowly nodded.

[28]

After Cueball left, Vivian sat down at her kitchen table and fished out a Virginia Slims cigarette. She thumbed a gold-plated cigarette lighter she kept close by on the marble-top table and breathed in the smoke and thought absently how there is no hit quite like the first one.

Her telephone rang. She picked it up.

"Yes?" After a moment, she replied to the voice on the other end, "No, Hub. Do not. And you stay out of my personal business. I won't have it."

The caller was not yet mollified.

Vivian DeMour's face reddened. Her jaw muscles filled out, as if she were clenching her teeth. Then a wild look flashed in her eyes, replaced by a stern coldness.

"Look here, Bailey," she hissed between clenched teeth. "I don't give a good crying damn about your problems with me or the way I conduct business, commercial or private. You are on my payroll, for the moment, because you are not so easily replaced. Bear that in mind for the future. At the moment, your star appears to be on the wane. It is up to you the direction it takes from here. Do I make myself clear?"

She hung up. She dragged on the cigarette once more and spun the package of cigarettes around between her nimble fingers.

The phone rang a second time. She answered it, her voice once again that of the pleasant yet businesslike woman. "Yes?"

As Vivian DeMour listened, she slid back in her chair, clutched the phone close to her ear, and breathed cigarette smoke to the ceiling between a wide smile.

"Oh, definitely. No, no. You were correct. A complete idiot. Always has been. He was just here."

She listened raptly, her smile remaining fixed. Finally, she interjected, putting a degree of sultry seduction into her voice, "Why don't you come over tonight, Leland? We can, uh, talk about it."

Vivian DeMour burst into laughter. She recovered quickly, took a quick drag of her cigarette and said, "Yeah. I have made some new additions to the boudoir. Have you ever done it under black light?"

• • •

Leland Morgan hung up the telephone.

"Bitch," he said.

From his third floor office, he gazed out the window to the blue waters of the Gulf of Mexico and the thin straight line of the horizon.

Morgan noticed his hand was trembling, and brought it up before his face. He turned it about as if seeing it for the first time, as if it were some alien thing he had never noticed before.

His phone rang.

"Morgan," he said, and listened. "Where?" He picked up a pen and began scratching on the note pad on his desk. "I'll be right down." He hung up.

"Shit," he said. "It never ends."

• • •

Leland Morgan pulled his car off Seawall Boulevard and into the sand. He drove between a pair of tall dunes and down to the beach below. A crowd was gathered. Fortunately the Galveston Police were already on the scene, having taped off the area with yellow crime scene ribbon suspended between four narrow steel stobs driven into the sand. The ribbon flapped in the breeze.

The sun was almost down. Hopefully the photography would begin before it was gone completely. You could never have enough good lighting at a crime scene.

"What we got here?" Morgan asked one of the uniformed officers and stepped over the crime scene tape.

"A couple of beach walkers found her. She hasn't been here long. The crabs hadn't gotten to her yet."

"Some looker," Morgan said, and regarded the body of the woman. "Geez. She got carved up, didn't she?"

"Yeah," the officer said. "Oddly enough, we've got her identity. That's her car parked over yonder. Her purse was still inside it and it was unlocked, so we found an I.D. that matches her face, so it's her. At least whoever did this didn't cut her face."

"Right," Morgan replied. "Any idea who did it?"

"We don't know anything yet. We do know she's not from here. She had lunch five hours hours ago at the Climax Club in Houston. Sounds like a real classy joint, to me. Found the receipt in her purse as well, with the time. It doesn't look like she had anyone with her when she came here."

"How do you know?" Morgan asked.

"When you see her car, you'll know. First of all, it's a piece of crap. Second, it's got all her worldly possessions in it. There's no room for anybody else to sit."

"Great. Yeah. I know what this means."

"We've got a killer loose on the Island," the officer said.

"Yeah," Morgan agreed, and sighed. "Yeah. We do."

"You know who did this, Lieutenant?"

"I think I do," he said. "And unfortunately, to catch him, I'll have to work with exactly the wrong people."

[29]

After a brief look at the murdered young woman in the Galveston County Coroner's Office, Cueball and Micah stepped out into the humid sunshine of a Gulf Coast morning. Leland Morgan followed them.

"This," Morgan said, "has taken on all of the earmarks of a serial killer on the loose. If it was Lynch, he sure changed techniques—he beats Jack Pense to a pulp, puts a bullet through Homer Underwood's head. Now he's graduated to knife work."

"He started with knife work a long time ago," Cueball said. "He used a knife in Houston and Dallas. Looks like he's gone back to that. Besides that, a knife is more...um...intimate."

"Why beat up Pense?" Morgan asked.

"I have no idea," Cueball said.

"You say she was a known prostitute?" Micah asked.

"Yeah," Morgan said. "She had the rap-sheet for it. She was originally from College Station, Texas. First busted when she was fifteen. She drifted down this way somehow and ended up getting picked up for soliciting in Fifth Ward, Houston. My guess is that her clientele were paying black men. But after a fine and a slap on the wrist later, she made her way here."

"A blond cutie like that a prostitute?" Cueball said. "She should have been in the movies. And with that name, Ivy Greene."

"Bad choices," Micah said. "We have to bring down the son of a bitch who did this."

Leland Morgan didn't answer. Instead he stood gazing out beyond the town and into the Gulf. "This badge says I can't kill someone unless I have to in order to protect others or myself. And then I have to."

"None of us wants to have to do that," Cueball said. "But we won't be killing Harrison Lynch. He's to be taken alive."

"Why is that?" Micah asked.

"I can't say just yet," Cueball stated. "Let's leave it for now."

Micah digested Cueball's words slowly. What was it he couldn't say? "We're a sad lot," he said. "We're dinosaurs is what we are. And we don't even know we're extinct. I tell you, gentlemen, I believe I would have no qualms whatsoever in taking that bastard out of this world. I believe I may have to do it, particularly after what I just saw. Because if I don't, I'm not sure I'll be able to live with myself."

"Micah," Cueball said. "You can ruminate on this all you want to. I've got to make a call over to the Galvez and set up an appointment. Check in on Jenny, see how she's getting on. If there's anything she needs, you let me know."

"Alright," Micah said.

"After you do that, would you drop in on Tommy Smart down at the pool hall and make sure everything's running alright down there?"

"Fine," Micah said. "Maybe by that time I'll find my appetite again."

"You do that," Cueball said. "Leland, you call me if you get any lead on Harrison Lynch. We'll do the same. It's the three of us in this together. Alright?"

Leland Morgan regarded Cueball. "Am I fostering your friendship enough now?"

"You're doing fine, Leland," Cueball said. "Just don't get too chummy. If you get in my way, I'll run right over you."

Morgan laughed. "Right. And I'd do the same to you."

[30]

After a leisurely breakfast on High Island the next day, Cueball and Micah hit the road to Beaumont and a visit to Denny Muldoon.

They pulled up at the curb on Harcourt Avenue in the shadow of a line of tall oak trees, some of which must have been pushing the two hundred mark age-wise.

Micah whistled. "Some spread," he said.

The estate sat on two perfectly trimmed and honed acres. A line of holly bushes phalanxed both sides of the fifty-foot long front porch. The columns were Corinthian.

"Makes me want to ask for a mint julep," Micah said as they stepped up onto the solid hardwood planks of the porch.

Cueball pushed the doorbell button. A buzzer echoed throughout the house.

After a bit, the massive front door opened. A short, thin woman of perhaps thirty stood in front of them. She had a swimmer's tan, curly tawny-brown hair, and blue eyes. She turned her attention from Cueball to Micah and smiled.

"Hello," she said. "My name's Minnie. Are you Mr. Boland and Mr. Lanscomb?"

"We are," Micah said. "I'm Lanscomb. This is Mr. Boland. Nice to meet you."

"It's nice to meet you too, Mr. Lanscomb. You're right on time. Won't you come in?" Minnie turned and the two men followed her.

Minnie led them from the foyer, with its polished mahogany, brass fittings and nineteenth-century crown molding and through a large dining room with a thirty-foot table laden with silver service and the obligatory chandelier. They passed the family room where a large fireplace stood with the ghosts of winters past hanging about, its screen closed and the ashes swept cleanly away. From the family room and down a long hallway the two men were led into what had clearly once been a combination den and library with floor-to-ceiling built-in bookshelves. The top shelves still held books, but the lower ones held hospital supplies. The room smelled of rubbing alcohol, antiseptic, and the unsettling smell of disease. On the raised hospital bed in the center of the room lay Denny Muldoon.

Minnie stepped beside the old man and spoke in a low whisper. His eyes opened.

"Ah-hmm," Muldoon cleared his throat. "Come in. Raise me up, Minnie. I recall asking you to have me dressed and in my chair before the visitors came."

"Yes, Denny," she said, not sounding the least apologetic about it. "But you were resting so quietly, and I thought they might not come after all. But here they are."

"Well, raise me up at least, dammit," the old man snapped.

Minnie pushed and held down a button on the side of the bed.

"How's that?"

"Fine. Now go away," Muldoon said.

Minnie brushed past Micah on the way out.

"So," Muldoon said, his voice a rasp and his eyes taking in the two men. "You two have a seat." There was a low settee close by.

"Now. How can I help you fellows?"

Micah tried propping one lanky leg up over the other but Cueball rapped his knee and Micah desisted.

"We want to know about Longnight," Cueball said. "Everything you know, if you care to tell it."

Denny Muldoon's eyes not so much closed as they appeared to sink back into his skull. He grimaced for a moment, then his eyes popped open again.

"Always and forever the past," he said. "Why do you want to know?"

"Because," Cueball said. "It's not over. It's happening again."

"Longnight is dead," Muldoon said. "And the world is safer. Unless crazy shithouse ghosts can kill from the grave, it's all over. It was over long ago, and all my nightmares are nothing but a dying man's inability to flush the past down the toilet. So tell me, please, why you would say such an impossible thing could happen?"

"Longnight's son is loose upon the world," Micah said. "And he's killing."

"In Galveston?" Muldoon asked.

Cueball nodded.

Muldoon stared at Cueball, then he looked away, his thin lips pursed in a flush of sudden anger.

Cueball continued, "I know that you and Bonaparte Foley were after Longnight. I know that Foley was told to put an end to the killings. Longnight never came to trial and the murders stopped. I would assume from these simple facts that you and Foley did your jobs."

Muldoon responded, "Foley was close on the heels of Longnight, and I had to divert him. I was under orders."

"From whom?" Micah asked.

"From J. Edgar Hoover. I was the closest agent to apprehending Longnight, and I was to turn him over to the OSS."

"OSS?" Micah asked.

"Office of Strategic Services," Cueball said. "Precursor to the CIA."

"Oh. Makes sense so far."

"I was afraid Foley was going to kill Longnight, even though he promised me he wouldn't. I couldn't trust him."

"Pardon me," Micah said, "but *you* couldn't trust *Foley?* Weren't *you* the federal agent?"

"Your friend doesn't like federal agents," Muldoon said to Cueball.

"No, he apparently doesn't," Cueball replied.

Muldoon laughed, and it sounded like an old hound dog barking. "Well hell, neither do I," he said. "I wish to hell I was the one who was taken off the case and Foley had found him first. Foley might have done the right thing and rid the world of him. Me? I was just following orders. That's exactly what those fellows said at Nuremberg right before they hung them—every single one of them."

Cueball nodded. "That's what they say."

"What did you do with him then?" Micah asked.

Muldoon grew quiet. He stared at Micah for a moment, as if seeing him for the first time.

"What value, I wonder, would you put upon an oath, Mr. Lanscomb?"

One of Micah's eyebrows shot up.

"What I mean is, after Minnie told me who was coming, I made a phone call," Muldoon gestured to the phone by his bed. "I found out who both of you were. You, Mr. Lanscomb, walked off from your job as sheriff with no more than a 'by your leave.' I'd say that there had to be a broken promise somewhere in there, no matter the circumstances."

Micah's lips compressed.

Cueball glanced at Micah sidelong and shook his head. *Don't say a word.*

"And you, Mr. Boland…The official line is that you retired as a Dallas cop and went into the security business. That's a bit of a stereotype, I know, but what's left out of that is your close association with Officer Hog Webern. Did you retire willingly, or were you forced out?"

Cueball didn't miss a beat. "I'll start double-dipping with my social security when I turn sixty-five. How about you? Living on family investments or something else?"

Muldoon laughed again and the old hound dog came out to frolic. The laughter, however, broke down into a fit of coughing.

"You see that bag at the side of the bed?" Muldoon asked, gesturing. "That one takes my urine. Then there's the machine over here that takes my blood and cleans it."

"Dialysis," Micah said.

"Right. And the government pays for the whole shootin' match. They pay for Minnie to take care of me too. And that's because I was the only man alive who could tell Longnight what to do. The only man he would listen to."

Cueball sighed. "You were talking about oaths."

"So I was. My oath was that I would never reveal to any living being any of the circumstances—or even the existence—of Longnight."

"Since there are at least two oath breakers in the room," Micah said, "if that's your contention, then you're outnumbered and at our mercy."

"Yes. I can see that. So I suppose I'll join you. From everything else I've learned about you two, I couldn't be in better company."

"Tell us then," Cueball said. "What was his real name?" Cueball asked.

"That's the one thing I won't tell you."

"Why?" Micah asked.

"First, because I promised, and that should be enough for you. Second, because no good can come from telling you."

"So be it," Cueball said.

Muldoon nodded and began. It took an hour for him to tell the whole tale, from start to finish.

"Can I ask you something?" Micah inquired when Muldoon seemed to be done.

"Go ahead."

"Did you know Homer Underwood back in those days?"

Muldoon's eyes fixed on Micah, and for a minute he stared at him, unblinking.

"Why do you ask?"

"Because. He seemed to know who you were."

"How is he?" Muldoon asked.

Cueball cleared his throat, interrupting. "Homer Underwood is dead. Murdered."

Muldoon accepted this bit of news quietly. He turned his head slowly and let out a long, deep sigh.

"A friend of yours?" Micah asked.

Muldoon didn't answer. Micah turned to Cueball, who quietly shook his head.

"Gentlemen," Muldoon said. "If you don't mind, I'd like to rest now. Would you please leave me in peace?"

Cueball and Micah stood, offered their thanks for the interview. Receiving no reply but a faint, curt nod, they filed out of the room.

• • •

Minnie escorted them back outside.

"Excuse me, Minnie," Micah asked. "We just gave Mr. Muldoon what appears to have been some bad news."

"Hmm. What was it?"

"We told him someone he once knew had died," Cueball replied.

"Who?"

"A man named Homer Underwood."

Minnie grew quiet.

"What is it?" Cueball asked.

"Mr. Underwood had been trying to contact Denny for years. I have always been instructed to turn him away and not relay his messages."

"Why?" Micah asked.

"I think something happened between the two of them."

Micah nodded.

Cueball turned to go, but Micah stood rooted to the spot, staring at the young woman. Cueball turned back and waited.

"May I call you later?" Micah asked her.

"Of course."

• • •

The long tale Denny Muldoon told Cueball and Micah that day was to be the last tale he told anyone. Denny Muldoon passed away two nights later. Micah received the news from Minnie. It was to be the first of many long conversations between the two.

SEPTEMBER 1944

[31]

There are few moments while in the midst of an unfolding catastrophe that are not surreal. The passage of time takes on a certain quality, a graininess of texture or flavor, perhaps not unlike the occasion of being mauled by a vicious animal or the headlong last-ditch flight to outrun a tornado. Some things in life are constant: water runs downhill, offal smells, and bad goes to worse in a twinkling.

Lyle Fisher and Big Bart Dumas stepped out of Lyle's '38 Ford panel truck onto the white rock driveway of the home on Broadway Street and into disaster.

"We going up and knocking on the front door?" Bart asked in hushed tones. The driveway was fifty yards long.

"Not exactly. I'm knocking on the front door. You're going around back. These are rich folks. They've got people who tend the garden, people who wash their cars...all kinds of people. Just act like you belong and everything will be fine."

"But I don't belong," Bart protested.

"This is just a friendly visit," Lyle said and winked at him.

As they approached the curve of the drive where it turned in front of the house, Lyle motioned Bart to head down the side towards the back. Bart shrugged and walked into the cool shade. He paused to see Lyle step up onto the long front porch with its ceiling fans and wicker furniture laid out like a parlor. Lyle motioned him on.

Bart passed a cistern which caught the runoff from the roof and resisted the urge to plunge his hands and face into the cool water. The aroma of baked pie assaulted his nose. His stomach rumbled. His hands shook. A rivulet of sweat went down his back and he shivered at it. This was to be no social visit, despite what Lyle had said. There would be no sitting on the veranda holding a fork just so. The infant was likely in one of the upstairs bedrooms, probably sleeping.

A sense of wrongness settled down upon his hulking frame like a well-worn cloak. It was a cold, enveloping thing. For some reason Bart thought about catfish.

At the rear of the house he paused and took a quick look around the corner. The back porch was screened-in, no doubt for those barmy nights when the mosquitoes took to hunting for blood in swarms. There was a clothesline twenty feet back of the front steps and there were diapers there. These diapers, however, appeared as though they were silk.

He heard the door chime then and forgot for a moment he had an accomplice. A woman's footsteps on hardwood floors came from within, going forward. Maybe the rear of the house would be vacant. This was his chance.

"Dammit," Bart breathed. "Dammit to hell. Here goes nothing."

He stepped around the corner.

As he went up the rear steps a voice called out from behind him: "Hey! What you doin' heah?"

Bart farted loudly. He turned to see a thin black woman with an empty clothes basket standing near the opposite corner of the house from which he had come.

"Uh. I'm, uh, going inside," Bart said, and then tried to smile.

"Wait!" the voice called, but Bart plunged on ahead. The screen door screeched open and he took four steps across the back porch—not gathering a single detail about the space—and went in through the wide-open rear door of the house, the air from his passage lifting the page of a calendar on the wall beside him. But there was no turning back. His body was a machine put into motion.

"Hey!" the voice called out in alarm, though still outside and somewhat muffled.

Along a hallway and past a kitchen, a narrow interior stairway beckoned. Up.

Into an ill-lit interior hallway on the second floor. He heard the screen door slam downstairs and knew it to be the maid he had ignored.

Within moments all manner of hell would come calling.

An open doorway and a quick peek inside. A wooden crib not far from a four-poster bed. No other person present. The walls of the elaborate crib were lined with quilts, all nice and comfy.

Across the floor to the crib. A pair of ice blue eyes greeted him. The child broke into a grin.

Bart picked up the kid and hefted him to his shoulder and turned to go. And at that exact moment he heard the shouting.

Down the hallway at a dead run, down the stairs.

"You're not going to take my baby!" he heard distinctly. A girl's voice, shouting. "Somebody! Help me! They're trying to take my baby!"

"Now hold on, Miss!" Lyle's voice, muffled, distant, attempting to reason. When he got to the kitchen, Bart heard the shotgun blast.

He took two steps toward the back door and stopped in his tracks.

"Lyle!" Bart shouted.

Silence.

He turned, shifted the kid from one shoulder to the other and ran in the direction of the gunfire.

He heard another scream, this one a woman's, and the front door of the house slammed and running feet pounded across the front porch outside. That would be the maid, Bart somehow knew.

It was all going so fast. Through a door, past a formal dining room and into a large living room.

A bad rendition of Lyle—like one of those department store manikins—lay sprawled across a burgundy, crushed-velvet settee twenty feet away. Lyle was riven and tattered from his right ear down to his chest. A girl—a young girl—stood close to him, her fist clutched against her lips. God, she was beautiful. The shotgun fell from her other hand to the floor. At that moment she sensed Bart behind her, turned her white-as-a-sheet face towards him to take in both his sheer size and the bundle he carried on his shoulder.

She screamed.

The infant at his shoulder clutched at his neck, hugging him.

"It's okay," Bart cooed softly to the child. He lunged forward just as the woman began to reach down for the shotgun again and he managed to kick it out of her hands so that it skittered across the floor and under the settee where Lyle lay bleeding out his life's blood.

"I'm taking him, girlie," Bart said. "Now stop screamin' and git, before I have to hurt you."

For a moment the girl simply stood there, dwarfed by him. Her mouth opened as if to reply, but then her eyes did a little dance in their sockets for an instant or two, and Bart was reminded of one of those one-armed bandits they kept in the back of the Balinese Room. Then her eyes rolled back in her head and she folded up and fainted.

"Goddamn," Bart said under his breath. He knew he had mere minutes to get going. But what to do? A baby at his neck, his co-kidnapper wounded and bleeding, a woman fainted dead away, a screaming maid right now running for the neighbors.

Lyle coughed and flecks of blood flew from his mouth.

"Come on, boss," Bart said. "We gotta get going."

Lyle tried to answer, but the words came out in a gargle of sound.

Bart reached down and scooped Lyle Fisher up with one arm around his waist and made for the large archway and the open front door beyond.

• • •

"The ferry," Bart said out loud as the wind whistled past. The turn-off toward the ferry was about twenty blocks north. A lone siren whined in the distance. "We'll never make it past the ferry, will we, boss?" He turned briefly to regard Lyle Fisher and found Lyle staring at him.

"Boss?" he said, but Lyle didn't blink.

"Oh no, boss. Not *now*. Not like *this.*"

• • •

Bart turned the truck onto a dirt road just before the ferry. Half a mile further on he found a lone pier with not a single living soul in evidence nearby.

He stopped the truck, patted the wailing child on the head, closed the door and went around and pulled Lyle's body out. Lyle felt like he weighed five hundred pounds, but he reasoned it was because he was "dead weight." He took him out onto the dock and dropped him into the surf to the side.

"I'm powerful sorry, boss," he said. The waters of Galveston Bay swallowed Lyle Fisher so utterly and completely that for a fleeting instant it was as if the man had never existed. But then after a minute the body came back up and lolled in the surf against the pilings beneath him.

And as Bart watched, the crabs came.

• • •

The ride home in Lyle's panel truck took ten minutes from the ferry to his driveway. They were the longest ten minutes of Bartholomew Elrood Dumas's entire life.

Quite fortunately neither his wife nor his brats were home to note either his condition or the nature of his luggage.

• • •

Having washed the blood from his hands and gotten the fire going in the trash barrel in the back yard, Bart chucked his bloody clothes into the fire, making sure none of his neighbors would be able to see what it was he was burning. For good measure, he threw the kitchen trash on top of it and the blaze grew merry, eating away the fuel with a hungry relish as only fire can.

He went back inside, donned a fresh shirt, checked on the baby lying on the couch—he was sleeping, as if nothing in the world had occurred—and then went back out front. He regarded Lyle's truck for a moment, then furrowed his brow and thought on it ever-so-deeply.

He walked over to the truck, opened it and fished around. Nothing. He opened the glove box. Nothing. He stepped back and regarded the interior. There was something behind the seat. He stepped forward and thumbed the latch that released the seat and it sprang forward. There was a paper sack there, one of those twenty-pound brown supermarket bags. He fished it out.

Inside he found fifty thousand dollars in hundred dollar bills.

Galveston, Texas

OCTOBER 1987

[32]

It had been a week since Micah and Cueball's visit to Denny Muldoon in Beaumont and five days following his death. The two men were still no closer to catching Harrison Lynch.

Rusty Taylor had the night off, his first in the last six months, and so Micah Lanscomb took the shift.

Micah tooled the Daihatsu pickup around the Island, varying his pattern as best he could, doubling back upon himself and turning off to distant checkpoints he had checked thirty minutes beforehand. Things had a tendency to fall into…less randomness. He was doing the best he could to defeat that and become completely unpredictable. You never knew who was watching a certain business, building or a warehouse, waiting for security to show up and then depart, not to be seen for several hours.

The moonless night was a black velvet blanket laid loosely over the island. There was hardly any breeze. The air was close, if a bit damp, as it ever seemed to be, and the temperature hovered around eighty degrees. Not enough to complain about, but just enough to make the brow bead with sweat.

The vision of Minnie's face—Muldoon's nurse—came before his eyes.

At times he tried to recall Diana's face from all those years before, but couldn't summon it. He had no pictures of her. He had nothing, no tangible thing from his old life. It was as if he had been reincarnated here on the island, yet into the same body, with full knowledge of his past existence—an existence he knew too well but couldn't properly recall. That existence had been the real life, and this current life just a shadow of it.

Not knowing exactly where he was going after he checked the southwestern-most account—a vacation home for one of Cueball's many friends that had been vacant for the greater part of the year—Micah found himself in front of a pay phone outside a convenience store.

He sat with his truck idling and the twin beams of his headlights illuminating the phone with its silvery cord. Maybe he'd be lucky and it would be out of order.

He turned off the motor and climbed out.

When he lifted the receiver, there was the resonating 'click' of the thing coming to life.

Micah deposited a quarter, fished her phone number out of his shirt pocket, dialed the number, then realized he hadn't checked the time. What was it? 1:00 a.m.?

"Hello?" the sleepy voice said.

"Hi," he said. "Minnie, this is Micah Lanscomb."

"Micah! Oh. I've been hoping you would call."

"I've been hoping I would too. I'm sorry it's so late."

"It's alright. I wasn't sleeping well anyway. And the house is different since Denny..."

"Yeah," Micah said, and then found he didn't really have much to say. "We must have talked for an hour the other night. I suppose I just wanted to hear your voice again. I'm selfish that way."

"Aw. That's the nicest thing anyone ever said to me. Denny's family is letting me stay here a few more nights, but then I have to leave. I suppose I'll find a place."

"Why don't you move to Galveston?" Micah asked. "There's nursing jobs here, I expect."

"Is that an invitation?"

"Yes. On behalf of the citizens and the Chamber of Commerce, I, Micah Lanscomb, invite you to Galveston."

"Thank you. You're a charmer, Micah. When can I see you?" Minne asked.

"I'd like for it to be soon," Micah said. "I'm on patrol right now. Working. But...the truth is I'm not sure I want you to be here on this island until we catch...until things have settled out."

"For my safety?" she asked.

"Yeah."

"How gallant."

There came one of those moments that was both interminable in length and yet not near long enough where the two of them were content to abide in the wake of each other's silence. Micah had only ever encountered a moment such as that twice before—the first when he was backstage after Diana's concert peering into her eyes just before he asked her out to dinner. The second was when he was contained within the well of his own silence beneath the sea, dying. It had been his first night on the island during the storm, and he had to decide whether to drown or to live.

"I'll call you when this business is over."

"You do that, Micah. I'll be waiting for you."

Silence again. Perhaps three minutes of it, if he had cared to glance at a clock.

"Goodbye, Minnie," Micah Lanscomb said.

"Goodbye, Micah," and it took her ten seconds to hang up.

DECEMBER 1943

[33]

Denny Muldoon was putting out the figurative fire that had erupted under him. The fire had a name, and that name was Robert L. "Bobby" Donnegal, the cabbie who had tipped off the local newspaperman, Homer Underwood, about the Mattie Wickett whorehouse murders.

At the moment, Bonaparte Foley was paying the cabbie a visit and attempting to put the fear of God into the man. It was the right kind of job for Foley too. Foley was all piss and vinegar and slow steam. The more subtle work, however, was Muldoon's strong suit.

"Can I get you something to drink, Mr. Underwood?" Muldoon asked, and made as if to open the bottom drawer of the desk. He had a bottle of Highland Scotch, placed there moments before his meeting with Underwood, but he wasn't too keen on sharing it. Anything, though, could be required to keep Underwood from running the story. The biggest piece of news was the murder of Bevo Martindale, one of the sheriff's deputies Longnight had cut to ribbons along with the whores. It wasn't that no one would care for the deaths of a few prostitutes and their madam. No. But Martindale was a big man locally. The story of Martindale's murder, along with the other victims, could potentially start a firestorm that would spook Longnight and make it impossible to catch the murderous son of a bitch. He could see the headlines already: BOGEYMAN STALKS GALVESTON! And with a second header proclaiming something like: POST OFFICE STREET MURDER SPREE COVERUP! Big news. Lots of papers sold. Five hundred or a thousand bogus phone calls per day jamming the Island switchboard.

"I don't drink so early in the day, Mr. Muldoon. Or is it 'Officer' Muldoon?"

"It's Denny. That's fine. It's too early for me too. I was just being neighborly."

"How can I help you, Denny?"

Muldoon sat back in his chair and regarded the man before him. Underwood wore a white cotton shirt and plain black suspenders. He had a cigar in his shirt pocket—probably waiting for a moment of privacy somewhere. Underwood knew why he was there. There was no hiding it on his face, although Muldoon could tell that the man was used to hiding a great deal. There was a hint of amusement there too, mingled with anticipation and quiet victory. He had a story to run. Perhaps the biggest story for the Island since the 1900 hurricane had wiped the place nearly clean.

"It might be a tall order," Muldoon said and let that sink in.

"Why don't you ask then?"

Muldoon leaned forward and placed his elbows on the desk in front of him. It was the police chief's office, and he had borrowed it from the man solely for this meeting.

"I'll ask then. Mr. Underwood, you sell newspapers. It's your job to print stories. So it is with some reluctance that I am forced to ask you to not do your job for a while."

"Beg pardon?"

"Really it's just the one story, and you know exactly what I'm talking about. Bobby Donnegal tells the story to his sister of what he finds one fine morning when he returns to Ms. Wickett's boarding house. The sister tells her best friend. This best friend happens to work for Homer Underwood at the *Galveston Daily News*. A few calls are made. Nope. No one has seen Bevo Martindale for some days. Nope. Ms. Wickett has closed her boarding house and gone off somewhere. But this story told by this cabbie, Donnegal? It starts getting bigger in the telling. Now there's talk of a Texas Ranger and an FBI agent. See what I mean?"

"You're asking me to kill a story? Seriously?"

"There's no story. There never was a story. I'll take you on a tour of Ms. Wickett's boarding house, if you are of a mind. You'll find nothing there, I assure you."

"What about Donnegal? Where is he?"

"Lord knows what cabbies do on their days off. Good luck finding him though."

Underwood smiled. He reached into his inside coat pocket and withdrew a square of hardback paper and laid it on the desk in front of him. It was a police photograph of Mattie Wickett's parlor, complete with the butchered hide of Martindale and two of the women.

"Name your price," Denny Muldoon stated.

"There ain't that much money on this island," Underwood stated.

Muldoon eased back in his chair and interlaced his fingers on top of his head.

"What if," he began, "and just 'what if.' What if the price had nothing to do with money?"

Underwood's eyes grew cool and steady. "Could you speak a little more plainly?"

"Plainly. All right. Try this. Name a thing."

"A thing," Underwood repeated uncertainly.

"Yes. A *thing*. It could be anything."

"Anything?" Underwood asked softly.

"Anything."

"Would you need to know now what that 'anything' would be?"

"No," Muldoon said, equally as soft. "You can think about it."

"I've already thought about it, Denny. I will accept your kind offer." Underwood stood up, plucked his hat from the corner of the desk and seated it on his head. "Tonight. The Hotel Galvez. Engage a room for the night. I will see you there at nine o'clock p.m. in the hotel bar."

Underwood turned to the door, opened it. Before leaving he said, "It'll be late enough then for us to have a few drinks."

Galveston, Texas

OCTOBER 1987

[34]

Cueball hadn't been inside the Galvez in years. Apart from its luxurious hotel suites and its spacious meeting rooms, the Galvez had a five-star restaurant that was one of the jewels of the Island. The grand Spanish architecture of the hotel extends into Bernardo's, the hotel's eatery, which is replete with vanilla linen tablecloths draped over hardwood tables from a century gone, candle-laden brass chandeliers and a panoramic view of the Gulf of Mexico. Cueball sat at a round table and finished off a glass of Italian wine.

"It is good?" the small man at his elbow inquired.

"Yes, Giuseppi, it is astonishingly good. But to me, any wine that I'm drinking is good. I told you before, I'm more of a whiskey man. You should save this for those customers more—"

"Particular, Mister C.C.?"

"Yes, Giuseppi. Particular I am not. Now," Cueball wiped his lips and laid his napkin aside, "you were going to give me the tour all over again."

"Yes, Mister C.C. Indeed!"

Giuseppi Grassi had come to Galveston in the early 1970s while Cueball was still a street cop in Dallas. The first night back on the Island, he and Myrna had stayed at the Galvez. Their realtor was getting the closing documents ready on their Ball Street house. Giuseppi had been no more than bellhop then, but over the years he had worked his way up into the hotel management. When Cueball had called the hotel asking for him, he was pleasantly surprised to have Giuseppi on the other end of the phone line in less than a minute.

During their stay all those years before, Giuseppi had made himself completely useful to Cueball, even going so far as to drive across town to fetch needed documents from his real estate agent. And during that stay neither Cueball nor Myrna had been ready for what Grassi called "The Grand Tour."

There simply hadn't been enough time back then. Cueball was glad Giuseppi was still here. He would now fulfill the little man's most fervent wish—or at least what had seemed so at the time.

"This way, Mister C.C.," Grassi said.

"Actually, Giuseppi, what I want is not quite what you call The Grand Tour. You've been around long enough to have heard all of the legends of this hotel, haven't you?"

Giuseppi Grassi stopped and turned toward Cueball.

"But of course."

"Then what I would like to see is the penthouse suite," Cueball said.

"Ahh! That. The home of Mr. Maceo."

"Yes. For starters."

"And then?"

"First the penthouse. The 'and thens' will all fall in line after that."

"Very good, sir," Giuseppi said and wheeled about. "To the elevator. Unless you would like to take the stairs?"

"I would, but my legs wouldn't. The elevator will do fine."

• • •

"There's nothing here," Cueball said.

"It is only a room," Giuseppi said. "Still, it is the best room in the place. See the view of the Gulf? And the roof terrace? This is a sought-after room. Presidents have stayed here."

"I wish the walls had ears," Cueball said. "And a mouth to repeat what was said."

"You are referring to Mister Maceo," Giuseppi said. "Perhaps you should speak with Mr. Blessing."

"Who?"

"He was here all those years ago, when Mister Maceo was here. He was a bellhop then. He comes to the restaurant downstairs for lunch, although he doesn't eat much when he does. His food is mostly wasted. I would like to introduce you to him, Mister C.C."

"I would appreciate that, Giuseppi."

"Maybe he'll be here today."

• • •

Cueball stepped around to face the man.

"Mr. Blessing?"

He was not much older than Cueball himself. His left side appeared more shrunken than his right, evidence of a stroke at some point within the last ten or fifteen years. The absence of muscle tone in his left arm, which rested atop his dinner napkin and the slackness of the left half of his face, giving him a lopsided, almost sardonic grin, bore testament to a sudden shift one day long before.

"Who are you?" the man asked, his words slow and deliberate as he looked up from his dinner, which looked as though it hadn't been touched. Blessing laid down the fork that he'd been holding in his right hand.

"I'm digging into Longnight."

"Longnight?" the man asked as he turned his eyes slowly toward Cueball. The man looked up at him and when he did, he shuddered.

"Longnight," Cueball said. "No one seems to know his real name. But I think you knew him."

"I haven't heard that name in a long time. Well, what are you waiting for? Have a seat."

Cueball sat to Blessing's right. "My name is C.C. Boland."

"What is it you want to know, Mr. Boland?" the stricken man asked.

"There's an entire history of this island that has never been written. It probably never will be written, thankfully."

"Brother, you can say that again. No one would believe it anyway, and it's best that way." Blessing tried to raise his left arm with his shoulder muscles, but gave it up and used his right hand to lift the lifeless, curled hand and place it on the table next to his plate. He leaned forward to keep it there.

"What do you want to know about Longnight?"

"How he was captured," Cueball said. "That for starters."

"It was me," Blessing said.

"I don't follow."

"There's that old saying about loose lips sinking ships."

"I'm familiar with it," Cueball said.

"Well, these old lips are about to start flapping again for you, Mr. Boland. Here, why don't you drink this glass of wine. They always fill one for me and I never touch it."

"Much obliged," Cueball said, and pulled the glass close to him.

"All right. It was 1943. And here's what happened."

[35]

"I was a young fellow then." Blessing began. "Sixteen or thereabouts. This was during the War. The rest of the world was going mad and here it was all light and glitter and fine wine. Sort of like they say the Titanic was before it went down. The island was a haven for anyone wanting to escape wherever they come from. I was a bellhop in this hotel we're sitting in when a strange man came. He was dark and suave and full of high intelligence. You could see things going on behind his eyes. He took it all in. I told him about the clubs and the girls and the nightlife.

"But this fellow, Longnight, he wasn't looking for whores. He was looking for…I didn't know what he was after, or, at least I didn't know at first. I pointed out the Balinese Room to him that first night, just across the street out his window. He spent a lot of time there at the Maceo's place—the Balinese Room—night after night after night. He was on the island from maybe October to December. He paid for his room in cash. He had one of those money belts they used to make and sell at the finest haberdashers. It was near to full when he got here and was only half empty by the time he was captured.

"The murders began within days of his arrival. I didn't connect any of that up until much later. First it was just disappearances. Someone whispering to me that so-and-so lady had up and left, I forget who, but she was the queen of the walk of high society. Another time there was a body found, or part of one, out on the beach just beneath the seawall. That sort of thing happens every once in a blue moon. But then there was the Post Office Street murders. That one got hushed-up. It never made the papers. In fact, none of it ever did. I think Homer Underwood managed to keep the story from getting out. He was the newspaper man in those days. But let me tell you, this island was stirred up. We were all nervous-like—the way you can kick an anthill lightly and watch those suckers come pouring out, running around in circles and madder than hell. One minute life goes on natural and normal, the next, the shadows at night begin to take on what they call 'definition.'

"But then that Texas Ranger fellow was on the Island and that federal agent. They were going here and there talking to people, asking questions. A lot of strange stuff started happening then. I seen Underwood and Muldoon, the federal agent, going into a room together and they didn't come out 'til the next day.

"One night I was working late and Longnight said something about going off in a direction he'd not gone before, so I had recommended a little club down on the west end. Hanny's Place. It was a colored joint with gambling going on that was sanctioned by the Maceos only so long as they paid-up properly. There was some wild stuff going on down that end in those days. Muldoon—that agent—he cornered me. He wanted to know where Longnight and Underwood had gone. Then he peeled out after them, and so I decided to follow him and see if he was going to kill them.

"Once I got to Hanny's Place—that was the colored joint—this black shape came around from behind me then and I like to have pissed my pants. At first I thought it was a ghost, but then I see it's the silhouette of a man in a cowboy hat. It was that Texas Ranger, Bonaparte Foley. He walks up to the front door and tries to open it, but by then those men already locked it from the inside. Then Foley takes his gun out and shoots the handle off the door, and then he shoots off the hinges. He took that door in his hands, threw it aside and stepped inside. I waited there in the dark, sweating the whole time but no one except Foley ever came out, and he came out alone. A bunch of white folks go into a colored joint? And don't come out? At first I thought maybe Foley had killed everybody in there. By this time I was out of my car and walking to the front entrance. Foley walked past me. I couldn't see much of his face because it was in shadow, but what I could see made me shiver all over. About that time I heard the sound of boat motors revving up ninety to nothing.

"When I went inside that place there wasn't a soul in sight. I didn't see any blood anywhere. No tables were turned over. Everything looked peaceful-like, as if everybody had been dancing and then got up and walked out, except I knew they had run. Even the musical instruments on the band stand lay there as if they had been put down calmly.

"I don't know what happened inside Hanny's place that night. Maybe there's no living soul who does know. But I do know this. No one ever heard or saw that Longnight fellow ever again. I heard that old Homer Underwood died recently. Muldoon too. Makes a fellow wonder who's going to die next. Yes. It does."

● ● ●

"Thank you for telling me everything, Mr. Blessing," Cueball said.

Blessing picked up his left hand with his right and put it back in his lap, then he regarded the plate in front of him as if seeing it for the first time. He lifted his right hand and pushed it away from him.

"Those days," he said. "There are times I wish I was back there. And then there are times I wish I'd never been born. But my daddy had a saying. He said, 'Wish in this hand, piss in this one, and see which one fills up faster.'"

"My daddy had almost the same saying," Cueball said, "only his wasn't as nice."

• *Galveston, Texas*

DECEMBER 24, 1943

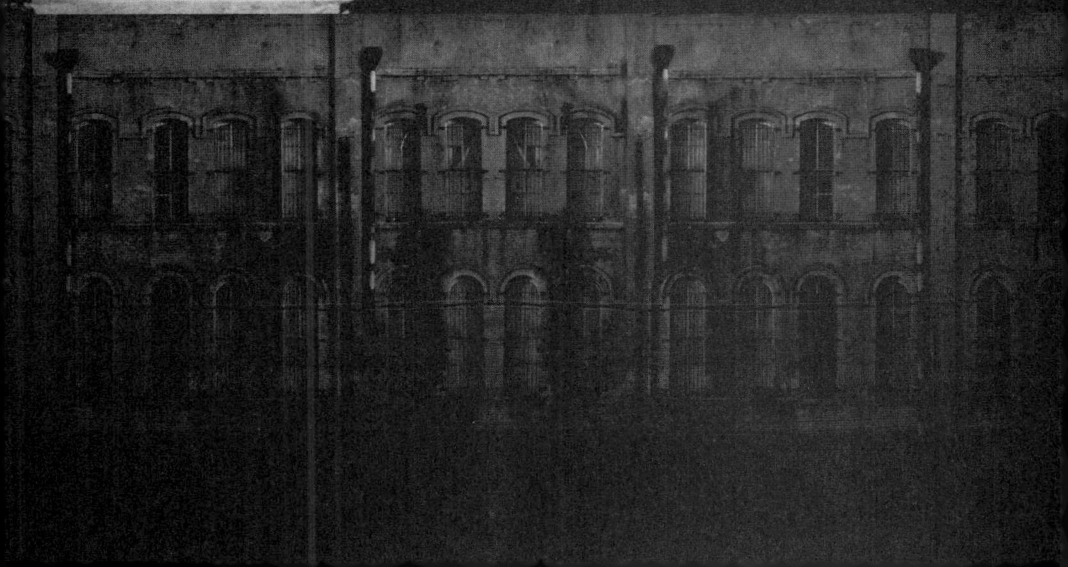

[36]

"Tad!" Denny Muldoon snapped across the lobby of the Galvez. The sun had gone down and the night had come. It was a warm night—too warm for Christmas Eve.

"Yes sir?" Tad Blessing asked.

"The dapper man. Where did he go?"

Blessing swallowed. "Uh…"

"Underwood went with him, didn't he?"

"Uh. Yes sir."

"Where?"

Blessing looked back toward the hotel front desk behind him to make certain they weren't being observed by the night manager. As he turned back he found himself being lifted off the ground by a fist knotted at his chest.

Muldoon pulled the kid's face close to his own. He reeked of alcohol, cigarettes and rancid sweat. He whispered to him between clenched teeth. "Listen, you little pissant nigger. You tell me where they went right this minute or I'll break your fucking neck."

Blessing nodded. He thought he might black out.

Muldoon set him down, released him and began smoothing his shirt and collar. He glanced over Blessing's shoulder and smiled at someone back there, either the consierge or the night manager.

"Okay," Muldoon whispered again, this time through a wide, false smile. "Where did they go?"

"Hanny's Place. Colored joint…on the west end. Sits out on a pier down there.

"How far down there? And how long ago did they leave?"

"About…eighteen miles. Half…half hour ago. Mr. Underwood and Mr. Longnight, they wanted—"

"What did you call him? *Longnight?*"

Blessing nodded.

"Shit," Muldoon said. He turned without another word and made for the front doors.

"Yeah. Shit," Tad Blessing said to himself.

• • •

Bonaparte Foley was hopping mad. A phone call to Austin during a rest stop in Houston quickly revealed that he had not indeed been summoned back as he had been led to believe. He'd called the governor's mansion and spoken directly with Governor Coke Stevenson. When Foley told the Govenor he was headed to Austin as fast as he could get there, Stevenson had said, "What's your hurry?" A moment of clarification had the governor asking him, "Just what the hell are you talking about, Ranger Foley?" to which Foley cryptically replied, "Apparently, Governor, I'm talking about a lying bastard of a federal agent. I'm sorry for the false alarm, Governor. And good night, sir."

Foley turned his Ford around and drove back to Galveston as if the four horsemen of the apocalypse were riding roughshod behind him. He had his mind made up to kill Muldoon long before he crossed the narrow corduroy causeway to the island.

Muldoon's car wasn't at the police station. On a hunch, Foley drove by the Galvez in time to see the bellhop, Tad Blessing, nearly wreck his car getting out of the parking lot. Blessing had neglected to turn on his headlights.

Foley turned into the Galvez, killed his headlights and then turned around and followed Blessing into the inky blackness.

• • •

It was obvious to Foley that Blessing was following someone else, and he had yet another hunch that it would be either Longnight or Muldoon. And Muldoon had been spending a great deal of time with that homosexual newspaperman, Homer Underwood. Underwood somehow must have Muldoon by the short hairs.

Foley drove by instinct and adrenaline alone. Blessing's occasional tap on his brakes was the only real clue how far ahead the kid was. In order to play it safe and avoid running into the kid's ass, Foley eased to the left and tried to stay in the oncoming lane, hoping no one else this night was driving without their headlights on this long, lonely stretch of Texas coast.

The trip took twenty nerve-wracking minutes. Foley watched as Blessing stopped his car across from Hanny's Place and just sat there in the dim lights outside the place. The parking lot at Hanny's was full, and the colored blues music from inside the place poured out into the stillness of the night.

Foley waited a minute to see if the kid would get out, but then decided to plunge ahead. One way or another, there would be some action. He'd either catch Longnight, or he'd catch up with Muldoon, or possibly *both* of them, and then there would be hell to pay.

[37]

Longnight was enthralled with the old colored man and his harmonica. As he watched him he unconsciously thrummed his fingers on the tabletop and tapped his foot against the hardwood floor of the place. The musician, all grizzled white hair over a taut, dark chocolate skeletal frame, made a rigid metronomic movement backward and forward to the bass drum beat. Shrill notes blasted from his harmonica between cupped hands in syncopation such that the damned thing seemed to speak, and what it orated was a tortured soliloquy of complaint against the world and the way things shouldn't be.

Blue smoke hung suspended just above head height. On the dance floor, the people moved and gyrated in a way Longnight had never seen before. It was alien and primal, and at the same moment raw and powerful. And it was, to his surprise, so completely *right*. Far from the class and style of the Balinese Room or the elegance of a grand ballroom, Hanny's Place was full of *life*. Young Tad Blessing had steered him to the right place. There was a twenty-dollar bill in the works for the kid when he got back to the hotel.

Longnight dropped a glance at Underwood. The man sat back in his chair across from him and likewise tapped the table to the compelling beat.

Underwood was a closet homosexual, this Longnight understood upon his first meeting with the man. It was plain to see in his face, if not in his mannerisms. He found Homer engaging and brutally honest, but for the necessarily secretive nature of his proclivitites. Longnight liked the man.

This was their third and final night out on the town together.

It had been a week since Longnight felt the hot blood on his hands. The Ranger and the FBI man were too close to catching him. It was his chance meeting with Underwood that had saved him. After a few drinks at the Balinese Room their first night on the town, Underwood leaned forward and whispered, "Can you keep a secret?" Pulling the rest of it out of him had been effortless. Underwood needed company—someone to talk to and who would listen, and who was above all his intellectual peer. The story came out in confidential whispers. Muldoon was an FBI Agent on the island tasked with finding the killer who had cleaned out Mattie Wickett's whorehouse. For some reason, Muldoon wanted to capture the man alive. Bonaparte Foley, on the other hand, was after blood. The fact that Muldoon had spilled all of his secrets to Underwood implied the existence of a relationship between the two men—likely a dangerous one. Their talk had almost certainly been pillow talk.

Longnight, to his credit, had listened raptly to Underwood, feigning disbelief where appropriate so as to draw out more and more information. That first night he was satisfied he knew all he needed to, with the exception of how close the two lawmen were to catching the killer. For that, another night on the town had been required.

This would be his last night in Galveston. Here, in Hanny's Place, he would listen to the music, breathe in the final quaff of cigarette-laden salt air. Later, when the two men returned to the hotel, Longnight would bid goodnight to Underwood and take a final stroll along the beach beneath the seawall in the dark and hear the waves break against the shore.

In the predawn hours he would take the Packard and drive west, leaving Galveston and the girl—the mother of his child to be. New Mexico and Arizona had loomed large in his thoughts of late, but the need to escape was far greater than the allure of mere exploration. He must leave the United States for good and all. Possibly he would turn south at El Paso and cross over into Mexico at Juarez. Central and South America beckoned to him. He would disappear, forever, into the night.

It was fitting. The night was his only true friend.

A shriek erupted from near the club entrance and the music ground to a halt.

Longnight and Underwood turned to look at the same instant.

"Oh shit," Underwood said.

Standing inside the doorway, thirty feet away, was Muldoon. And he had a gun in his hand.

• • •

The crowd began pouring out of the front entrance. The band laid down their instruments carefully. The old black harmonica player sat in his chair and regarded Muldoon. After a moment he looked over to Longnight and Underwood, who likewise kept their seats. The old man nodded to the two men and then gestured toward Muldoon, as if to say, "This is your problem, not mine."

Another man stepped up beside the harmonica player. Longnight pegged the man for Hanny, the place's namesake.

"I'm Hanny Blake. Guns aren't allowed in my club."

"Out," Muldoon said.

Hanny looked to Underwood and Longnight. Underwood nodded.

"If there's any damage to my club, I'll demand to be reimbursed for it." Homer nodded again.

Hanny helped the muscian down from the stage and they made their way out the front door.

The room was empty and motionless, but for the slowly revolving ceiling fans. Most of the smoke had left with the crowd. Muldoon waited until Hanny and the musician exited and closed the door behind them. He turned the door lock and slid the bolt home.

Muldoon walked over to Underwood and Longnight's table.

"Why don't you have a seat, Denny?" Homer said.

"Is this your new flame?" Muldoon asked Underwood and gestured to Longnight.

"Flame? Oh!" Homer laughed. "No. This is my friend. Mr. Talos, this is Denny Muldoon. He's FBI."

"It's nice to finally meet you, Mr. Muldoon," Longnight said, and offered to shake hands. It created an awkward moment of long silence. It was clear Muldoon wasn't the least interested in shaking anyone's hand. To add to this, Muldoon's right hand held a revolver of some large calibre. The gun, however was still aimed at the floor.

"Do you have any idea who this man is?" Muldoon asked Underwood.

"He's my friend. That's all I need to know."

"Talos, huh?" Muldoon said, managing a gruff laugh through his glowering countenance. "His friends, though. They call him by his nickname. They call him Longnight."

In the speechless silence that ensued, the three men heard the report of a gun going off outside. The inside door handle skittered across the empty dance floor trailing splinters of wood.

It was Muldoon's turn to say it.

"Shit."

• *Galveston, Texas*
OCTOBER 1987

[38]

"There is no way in hell," Cueball said, "that I'm going to let you use Vivian DeMour as bait."

"Not me," Micah said, "Us." He took a forkful of pancake and tracked it through the small harbor of syrup on his plate.

"Not you, not me, not anybody," Cueball said. "We could wind up getting her killed. It's too much of a risk."

"So is letting Lynch go on killing," Micah said. "I need you to listen to me for once, C.C."

"Alright," Cueball said, his arms braced against the bar. Micah sat on a barstool opposite him and gobbled his pancakes. It was the way Micah did everything—with a quiet yet rapid relish. "I never said I wouldn't listen to you. That I'll do. But I do reserve my veto power."

"Fine," Micah said. "Now, let's assume that Lynch has figured out that Lindy DeMour was his mother. He knows she's dead. Also, he must know by now that Longnight is his father. That explains all the correspondence with Hub Bailey, the fact that the DeMours have been paying for all the silence about their relationship with a killer by keeping his prisoner account full."

"How do you know about that?" Cueball asked.

"Found that out from Hub Bailey. By the way, I had to make up a little white lie. Something about fifty-thousand dollars dropped off to you in cash from someone in the State House. The refund from Lynch's prisoner account. Remember Sheer saying Lynch had that much in his commissary account."

Cueball laughed. "I'll have to figure my way around that one when he comes asking for it. But do go on."

"So. Lynch thinks he can wipe out the DeMours. Maybe he imagines he can come into the family money. I think he was trying to get to the family papers when he opened that safe after he killed Jack. I think he forced Jack to tell him everything he knew, including where the family papers may have been. Then he killed him."

"That makes sense," Cueball said.

"And there's only one way I know of to make him come running."

"Vivian."

"Yeah." Micah said, "And to do this right, we'll have to get word to Hub Bailey that Vivian DeMour is meeting you to pick up the fifty thousand dollars in person. I can tell Bailey that you decided to go around him and take the money directly to Vivian."

"All this presupposes that your buddy Hub Bailey is feeding information to Harrison Lynch," Cueball said.

Micah was mildly surprised his boss had let him get so far along with this particular line of thought. He decided to press onward and damn the torpedoes.

"How else could Lynch know within a day of getting to the Island where the family papers would be, where Jack Pense was, and maybe even how to find Homer."

"I'll be damned," Cueball said and slapped the counter with one meaty hand. "There seemed a little too much coincidence all along here. Jack Pense was on my payroll and guarding a warehouse owned by the DeMours. It wasn't just a safe and a warehouse. It was *the* safe in *the* warehouse."

"Right," Micah said.

"Okay. Go on."

"So to do this right, we need not only Vivian, we'll need you and me and we'll need somebody I sure as hell don't relish including. Our other musketeer."

"Leland Morgan," Cueball said. "And the Galveston police force."

"Right. We'll need some backup for this operation."

• • •

Micah left for the ASG building.

When he got there, Hub Bailey was doing some filing. From what Micah could gather, the entire third floor filing room, a good chunk of the third floor space, was Bailey's own bailiwick, and he didn't trust anyone to file anything for him. Micah had met people like that before: methodical to a fault.

"Mr. Bailey?" Micah called back into the dim space.

"Hello! Back here!"

"It's Micah Lanscomb."

Bailey's glasses were pushed up onto his forehead. He had a stack of papers in his hand. He was sorting them into a row of smaller stacks on a tabletop in front of a long row of four-drawer file cabinets.

"Oh! Mr. Lanscomb! I was hoping you would come by. I hope you brought a check with you."

"No such luck," Micah said. He positioned himself opposite Bailey with the table between them. "It appears that Mr. Boland is delivering the money to Ms. DeMour himself."

"Oh my God! He mustn't do that. She'll only make matters worse."

Micah had to suppress a smile.

The man was clearly agitated. He dropped the stack of papers on his desk and started to walk away, but then turned and regarded Micah as if seeing him for the first time.

"When is this meeting supposed to occur? And where?"

• • •

The sun was hidden behind a bank of clouds that outlined the Island in shadow. The Gulf gleamed brightly. Leland Morgan pulled up in front of Nell's Diner and nodded to Cueball and Micah through the plate glass window.

He came in and took a seat. Micah handed him a menu and Morgan batted it away. Cueball laughed.

Nell came over and took their orders anyway. Then she disappeared into the kitchen.

"I want your assurance that Vivian DeMour will not be in any danger," Cueball said.

"My men will be watching. Archie Ransom will be on the roof of the automotive store next door."

"The sharpshooter?" Micah asked. "Good. I like that fellow."

"No," Cueball said. "No sharpshooter. No shooting Lynch."

"I don't get you, boss," Micah said.

"You don't have to. All you have to do is what I say. And Morgan, are you and I also clear on that?"

"Clear as can be. But I want to know why."

"Maybe after this is all over, I'll tell you. Not now. And just so we have all this straight, Viv is to pull up to the motel room door, get out, unlock the door and go inside."

"Right," Morgan said. "She'll be wired and she'll be listening and we'll tell her if it looks clear for her to do so."

"What if you see Lynch?" Micah asked.

"I'm counting on that," Cueball said. "I'm going to be there."

"My initial plan," Morgan said, "was that if we were to see Lynch first, we would take him down. Now you're changing all that. It makes the whole situation far more dangerous. For my men, for you and Micah, and for Ms. DeMour."

"I don't care what you think about this or anything," Cueball said. "That's the way it's going to shake down."

"Why not just shoot him through the heart?" Micah asked. "Or the head?"

"Shut up, Micah," Cueball said. "The subject is closed. Alright, Morgan, so the minute Viv goes inside, what's your plan?"

"I'll have my men inside. They are to get her into the bathroom and close the door. She'll be shielded there."

"Your men will be in the room?" Cueball asked.

"They'll be there."

"Good," Micah said.

"You going to pin Lynch for killing Jack Pense?" Cueball asked.

"It's a done deal. The District Attorney is preparing the indictment as we speak. I'll have the warrant in the next couple hours."

"In my experience," Cueball said, "the first casualty in any battle is always the plan of battle. You just protect Vivian, Leland. If anything goes wrong, I'm holding you personally responsible."

"What would you do to me, do you think? Feed me to the crabs?" Morgan chuckled.

Cueball fixed Leland Morgan with a cold stare. "That sounds far too merciful compared to what comes to mind."

[39]

"I never did have any use for waiting," Micah said.

"You want to go get him right now? He's got to take the bait we've offered. If we screw this up, he walks. But you know that."

Micah leaned forward and pressed his head into his hands. The sun was beginning its downward climb somewhere behind the house. The shadows in the front yard lengthened.

"I need to replace that bulb over there," Cueball mumbled to himself.

"How do you do it, C.C.?"

"Do what?"

"Just sit there and think about replacing light bulbs?"

Cueball ran one leathery hand along his jawline. "I'm just like you and everybody else," he said. "I don't like waiting either, but when a fellow has got to do something he had better get after it, whether it's waiting, dancing or playing mumble-peg."

"Or killing," Micah said.

"Or killing," Cueball said. "Which, in this case, is *not* going to happen."

"I still don't understand it," Micah said and ran his hand through a long shock of hair, wiping away the sweat.

"Why don't you go home and get some sleep. I can call you when the time comes. There's several hours left to go and one of us should get some sleep. Five-thirty a.m. comes early."

"Can't," Micah said. "Too keyed-up."

"Well then, why don't you go out? You know? It's only eleven o'clock at night. You could find a nice young filly somewhere and—"

"Sow some wild oats?" Micah finished for him.

"Something like that. Or not. Hell, I don't know and I don't care. But anything beats watching you punish yourself since time immemorial. You need a woman, Micah. A good woman. There *are* some still out there. Women like that Minnie. Muldoon's nurse."

"Now how the freaking hell did we get on this topic?"

"It always comes to it," Cueball said. "Women." Cueball took a long pull on his glass, eased back and sighed.

Micah paused, letting it soak in. He thought of a reply, then thought better of it.

"You know," Cueball began, almost offhandedly, "you never told me the whole story about you. And Diana."

"Yeah. I know. There's only that one girl for me, and she's resting right now."

"In a cemetery, my friend. In a *cemetery*."

"Doesn't matter."

Cueball twisted the lid off the bottle and filled Micah's cup.

Micah studied the filled glass. He picked it up, drained it in one long pull, and sat back, waiting for the world to begin spinning. When it didn't, he laughed out loud.

"Okay, C.C.," he said. "I'll tell you. Your damned eternal patience is an abomination before the sight and mind of God."

So then and there the story came out—about how a wandering man, stranger to his own home and life, trekked across America in search of... something. About how he found comfort and solace when he returned home in the arms of a Juilliard harpist. The story came from the tall, wiry man without any recrimination, without tears, and without a break. To his credit Cueball Boland listened to every word. By the time he was done, it was time to get ready for their early morning appointment.

[40]

Micah Lanscomb had brought more guns with him than the two of them would ever need, including a Remington 12-gauge riot gun, his first pick, an AMT Hardballer .45, satin-finish, adjustable trigger pull, triple-safety. After that there was the Remington 22-250, a deer-rifle/sniper rifle with the Starlite scope. And one of Micah's favorite guns—a British .303 Enfield. A beauty of a rifle, the wood polished so that the tawny-brown grain had a lustre to it and the black, hardened steel smooth and cold to the touch. A gun without remorse, without conscience. A killer of a gun.

Micah was hoping he would get the chance to take down Harrison Lynch. Cueball or no Cueball.

Cueball Boland was sitting in his truck when Micah pulled up. "We won't need any of this firepower, Micah. Like I said before, no one shoots Harrison Lynch."

Micah didn't comment.

• • •

The parking lot was empty, except for a lone sedan parked down at the end. That would be the room that Lynch would enter.

The Bayside Motel had seen better days. In its tourist court heyday, it had seen the likes of musicians who played at the Balinese Room and even in the clubhouse at the Galvez. Ultimately, it had made its money when the big hotels were full in a time when the Island was packed shoulder-to-shoulder and there was spillover to be had. Now it was a seedy, shabby, run-down shadow of its former self, a haven for transients.

Cueball and Micah parked at the small lumber supply place next to the motel, got out and walked around the corner of the building where they could see the street and part of the Bayside parking lot.

"I'm in favor of waiting in shadow until he walks up to the door," Micah whispered. "Then we can get the drop on him from safety."

"Hell," Cueball said. "Something's already gone wrong."

"What do you mean?"

"Look around you. Do you see any evidence whatsoever of Leland Morgan or any of his men?"

Micah scanned the area. Nothing.

"Follow me," Cueball said. He stepped the length of the supply store front walkway and paused at the corner.

"That's Vivian's car," Cueball said. "Aw hell. She's early. But I don't see anybody else here." Cueball fumbled for his radio and keyed the mic.

"Morgan?"

Static came back at him.

"Morgan, if you don't answer me in about ten seconds, we're going in there. Viv's car is here. She's early."

More static.

"It's your call, boss," Micah said, and pumped a round into the chamber of this shotgun.

"Hell," Cueball said and threw down the radio. "I don't like this one damned bit. Something's bad wrong. Let's go."

Cueball stepped into the grass ditch between the lumber supply store and the motel parking lot, which was empty but for Vivian's sedan.

"I'll kick the door in," Micah said.

The two men stopped fifty feet away from the motel room door. A bare bulb glared underneath the eaves above the door.

"You'll kick it," Cueball said, "but if it doesn't cave, I'll shoot the doorknob off."

"There'll be a chain on it at the top."

"Doesn't matter," Cueball said. "I'll blow it off if I have to. Hand me that 12-gauge."

Micah traded guns with Cueball.

• • •

Cueball stood to the side while Micah balanced on one leg like a karate master. He tucked the other leg up close to his torso, spun three-sixty and struck the door near the knob with the tip of his boot, bringing all his weight and muscle to bear. The door slammed open and Cueball rushed in ahead of Micah.

The light was on in the room and there were four men. All four looked up in alarm.

Cueball recognized Harrison Lynch, sitting in a chair away from a folding table, his hands behind him as if he were handcuffed. Lynch's face wore a look of insane glee. His sandy blond hair swept back from his face sprouting from a distinct window's peak. It was the same man Cueball had busted all those years ago in Dallas, but this man was in his early forties now. No longer a punk kid.

"Who the hell are you?" Cueball asked, raising the barrel of the shotgun and aiming it at one of the men who had begun to rise to his feet.

"Hello, Mr. Boland, Mr. Lanscomb. My name is Shane Robeling. FBI."

"Bullshit," Micah said.

All of the men at the table began to reach slowly for their identification. Cueball noticed the stenciled "FBI" on each of their jacket breasts.

"Not so fast, gentlemen," Micah said. He had Cueball's Mauser in his hand and from his stance and the way he trained it on the men he meant business. The FBI agents slowly withdrew their hands.

"I don't know if I'd threaten a federal agent, Mr. Lanscomb," Robeling said. "The penalties could be...severe."

"What the hell is going on here?" Cueball asked.

"We've got the man everybody is after in custody," Robeling said. "Without his knife I believe he's quite harmless." Robeling put his hand out to the table and picked up a knife and showed it to Cueball and Micah."

"That looks like it could be the knife, alright," Cueball said. "It's the one he used on a young prostitute named Ivy Greene. So what's your plan?"

"That's none of your concern," Robeling stated.

"Like hell," Micah said. He took a step forward and swiveled the Mauser to cover Harrison Lynch.

"You can't shoot him, Mr. Lanscomb. You can't kill a man like that in cold blood."

"You'd be surprised at what I can do," Micah said.

"Micah," Cueball said softly.

But Micah's back was to Cueball and to the other men in the room now. From two feet away he centered the barrel of his gun on Lynch's forehead.

Micah Lanscomb had reached a crossroads in his life. After a lifetime of wandering across the country from ocean to ocean, looking for something, he had finally found it. It was there in the mad eyes of Harrison Lynch. He looked into those eyes and saw the body of a young woman named Ivy Greene. The young prostitute faded from view to be replaced by the savaged form of Susan Glover, torn and bloody on a California night all those years ago. It may as well have been yesterday.

"Micah," Cueball stated. "Don't."

Lynch grinned up at Micah.

Micah heard something else then. He heard the sound of the surf. It was far away at first, as if it was outside the open door and across the street, but then it grew loud in his ears. Waves crashed over him and his lungs felt deprived of air. He wanted to die, yet something inside him desperately wanted to live. His throat tightened into a ball.

Micah Lanscomb slowly closed the distance of his gun barrel to Harrison Lynch's forehead until it made contact.

"This is how I live," Micah said, and squeezed the trigger.

• *La Marque, Texas*

SEPTEMBER 1944

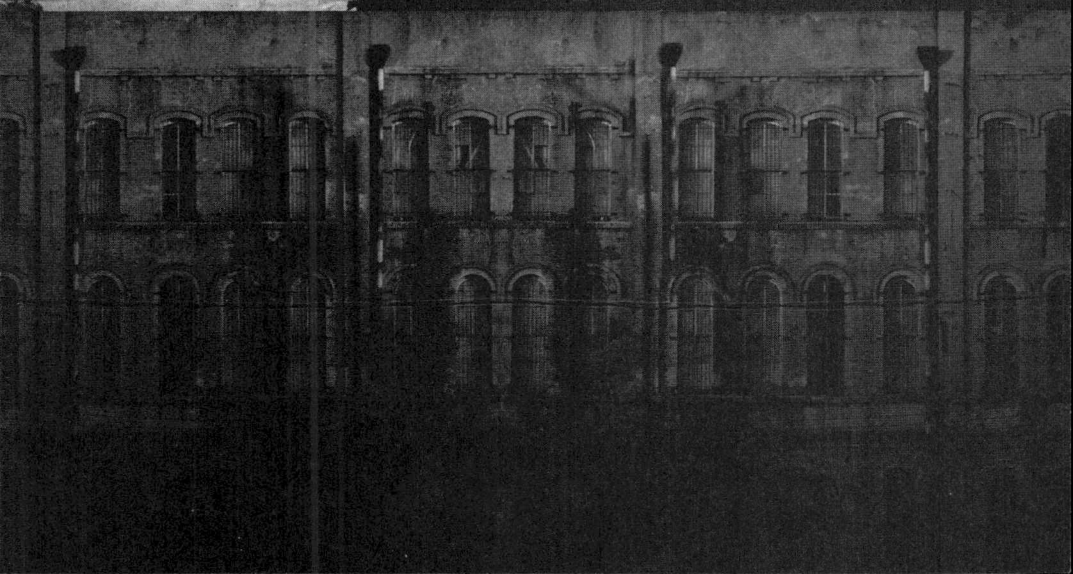

[41]

Big Bart was drunk, and it wasn't a Friday night. He hadn't been to work. He hadn't even left the house. Instead he'd sent Jacky, his eldest son, two doors down to the grocery store with a note for Mr. Roddingham and a hundred-dollar bill. The kid returned with the package ten minutes later and Big Bart set to drinking.

The new kid cried a lot. He wailed. He shrieked. When Lorraine finally got up the nerve to demand Bart spill the story to her—the mystery of how the kid came to be with them, what was going on with his job, the whole works—he ignored her. Instead he went outside and took to breaking a row of sod with his hoe. He was finally going to put in the garden he had been promising her in their postage stamp of a back yard.

Bart's head pulsed with streaks of pain like fingers of red lava flowing uphill and he thought about his father, who had dropped dead of a heart-attack at the age of thirty-nine. He felt something stinging at his ankle and looked down and realized he couldn't see his feet because his gut was in the way.

"Maybe I oughta do somethin' 'bout that," he said to himself.

"Just relax," a voice said, "there ain't a thing to worry about."

It sounded like whoever had said it had been standing right there next to him, but there was positively no one around. A cold shiver took hold of him, made little needle-like prickles in his gut and on the nape of his neck.

The voice had been that of Lyle Fisher.

"Good sweet Lord, I'm goin' plain goofy," he said after half a minute of complete stillness and silence.

The image came full-blown over the rest of the world around him: Lyle's lifeless eyes staring into his, as if he understood Bart even in death. The blood no longer oozed from his shoulder, neck and jaw. Instead it congealed there.

"I'm powerful sorry, boss," Big Bart stated to the memory.

"It's alright," the voice said, and for just a moment the lips in the image moved along with the voice. "I was going to cheat you out of your fair share anyway."

"I knew," Bart said. "I knew it the minute I found that sack."

Bart reached over to retrieve the bottle from the grass where he had hidden it from Lorraine's prying eyes behind a patch of weeds. He scanned the back windows of the house for her accusative face. Finding her somehow less-pretty face absent, he uncorked the bottle and took a long pull of whiskey. It burned hard going down and after a moment took away the edge of the continuous throb going on in his head.

"That better?" Lyle asked.

"Yeah. Amen to that. Sure wish I could see you, boss."

"You got a problem, Bart," Lyle said.

"I don't drink too much," Bart said, growing slightly angry.

"I'm not talking about your drinking. I'm talking about the fact that half the State of Texas is looking for that little rich kid. You haven't bought a newspaper lately, have you?"

"What in the hell would I need a newspaper for?" Bart asked. He put the bottle back down behind the weeds and commenced hoeing again. If he had bothered to look, he would have seen that his furrow was beginning to assume the shape of a horseshoe.

"If you had a newspaper, you'd know," Lyle said. "Makes a fellow wonder whether any of your neighbors read the paper."

Bart stopped, suddenly. Another set of shivers overcame him. His eyes did a little dance for a moment, as if following some unseen will-o-wisp, then, just as quickly he threw down the hoe and walked towards the house.

"Don't bother to wait for me," Bart said over his shoulder.

• • •

When the screen door to the kitchen slammed, Lorraine Dumas instinctively clutched the child to her hard. She waited for him to let out a wail as she overcame the shock.

"Give me the kid," Bart snapped.

"You're drunk! You can't have no baby when you're drunk. You get out of here Bartholomew. You git!"

"It ain't safe havin' him here, Lorraine. I got to do what Lyle was gonna do, whatever that was."

"And just where is Lyle, Bartholomew? Huh? You answer me that?"

"Lor-RAINE! You better give me that baby. He ain't safe, I tell you!"

"You tell me where you're taking him and maybe I'll go along and hold him. But I ain't letting you touch him till you're sober. And that's the final word on it."

Her voice had gone quiet. Soft, in fact, but she spoke through clenched teeth, and to Bart's ears it was the most savage sound he had ever heard.

"Alright," he said. "Alright already. You hold him. Send the kids to the neighbors or somethin', but we got to get him outta here."

"It's been nearly two days and now you finally say it. This is the DeMour baby, ain't he? Which means you're going to prison."

"I ain't going to prison. What I did was the right thing. And if you knew why, you'd have gone along with it."

Lorraine was through talking, this Bart could tell.

"Get your keys," she hissed at him and he winced. "We're taking him somewhere, all right. You mind what I tell you and maybe you won't wind up in prison. Men! Always have to do their thinking for them."

And with that Bart withdrew from the kitchen.

• • •

When Bart walked out of the house fifteen minutes later behind his wife who was holding the kidnapped child and had his own two children in tow, he looked back for a moment, almost expecting to see Lyle Fisher standing there on the porch. Instead all he saw was a cock-eyed porch and a house that needed a coat of paint.

"Maybe when we get back," he said to Lorraine's back, "I'll do something to fix up the house. Or maybe we'll get a new one."

But Big Bart Dumas never came home again.

• Galveston, Texas

OCTOBER 1987

[42]

There was a sharp clicking sound and then Harrison Lynch's head did *not* form a black hole.

An instant later the gun was wrenched from Micah's hands.

Micah turned to look at the man who had taken the Mauser from him. It was Cueball Boland.

"I had to make sure, Micah," Cueball said. He handed the Mauser to Robeling. "I'm sorry, but I made a promise."

Micah looked down at his hands. He had never studied them before. He had always thought he had hard hands, but these strange appendages looked smooth and soft.

"I changed guns with you because I loaded mine with dummies. In fact every gun you brought was probably loaded with cartridges with no powder in them. I did it yesterday, as soon as the meeting was set up. I had to be sure, though."

The shock on Micah Lanscomb's face did not fade. His ears were still full of ocean water. His breath came in hitches.

"Fellahs," Cueball said. "Get my friend a chair. And a glass of water."

Micah Lanscomb found himself sitting and staring at an empty bed.

"It's over," Cueball said.

• • •

Micah was nearly back to reality by the time Harrison Lynch was led from the motel room by Robeling's men. An FBI van pulled up in front of the open and permanently damaged motel room door and Lynch was placed inside. A moment later the van pulled away. Micah sat in silence and watched it go.

"One of my men took Ms. DeMour home right after Lynch arrived. So you can stop worrying about her," Shane Robeling said.

"Why didn't she drive?" Cueball asked.

"Because Lynch slit a couple of her tires before entering. We're pretty sure he was going to kill her. And let me tell you, I never saw a woman who wanted to get herself killed more than that one. She had to be restrained when we put the cuffs on Lynch. I thought she was going to take us all on."

"That must have been a sight," Cueball said. "First things first: why didn't you warn us that the FBI was swooping in to capture Lynch? We wouldn't have busted down the door and very nearly gotten somebody, including ourselves, killed."

"You *were* warned," Robeling said. "I'm surprised you didn't get your heads blown off for that stunt."

"No," Micah said. "Didn't happen. We weren't warned." He had recovered, mostly, although there was still a faraway look in his eyes.

Robeling looked at the two men quizzically. Then he sighed and grinned.

"What?" Cueball said.

"Well, I'm hesitant to say."

"You don't have to," Micah said. "I've already figured it out."

"Morgan," Cueball said, having arrived at the same conclusion.

"That's right," Robeling admitted. "We detained all of Morgan's men a few blocks from here, took away their guns and their police radios, just so that no one could be tipped off. Morgan told me about you and Lanscomb, so I ordered Morgan to let you know we had taken over and call you off. I handed his cell phone back to him for a moment, he walked away to make the call, then came back and said it was all arranged."

Cueball gritted his teeth.

"It changes nothing," Robeling said. "Lynch is in custody, on his way to Virginia at the moment."

"You mean," Micah Lanscomb almost spat the words, "that you and the government are going to keep this cold-blooded killer?"

Robeling had asked the other agents to leave the motel room, and it was just the three of them now sitting at the card table. The light of day was coming up outside, and the men could see it leaking through around the pulled drapes.

"Mr. Boland," Special Agent Robeling said, ignoring Lanscomb, "you know as well as me that's what governments do."

"There's no need to preach to me," Cueball said. He now seemed far calmer than Micah Lanscomb, for one, and himself, for another, would have believed. "But this man has no use."

"I don't know about that," Robeling said. "But then again, I'm not the policymaker here."

"Who is?" Micah asked. For a moment he was certain that Robeling was going to continue ignoring him, but instead he turned to face the perplexed man.

"Let me tell you something, Mr. Lanscomb," Robeling began and put on his most patient and bored face. "Some men go through college and work all their lives to make one little breakthrough that will likely be completely unappreciated in their own time. For instance, there is a professor I know of down at Texas A&M—he's a simple soul. A farmer. But *man,* can he grow things. Well, this guy has given the world crops that grow in soil that's practically rock. He's produced more strains of food than you or I could ever name. And you know what? Nobody knows his name. Hell, right now I can't even think of it. But he's the Einstein of the agricultural world."

"You can't be comparing your professor to Harrison Lynch," Cueball stated, calmly.

"I'm not, as far as what Lynch has done. I am, though, as far as what he's capable of."

"Mr. Robeling," Cueball said. "My friend and I are all ears right now. Why don't you cut to the chase and tell us."

"Alright then. Cryptanalysis is a very old science."

"So?" Cueball said.

"No one has ever come up with a code that couldn't be broken. A code, a cipher, as they call it, is a finite thing, and any finite thing has—"

"A pattern," Micah interjected.

"Hush," Cueball said.

"Parameters," Robeling continued. "But there are some in the government who believe that a cipher without parameters could exist. Lynch is a mathematician. The best."

"Please don't tell us that you want him to create the unbreakable code," Cueball said. "I don't think I could live with this man walking for the sake of such a silly thing."

"Silly?" Robeling said. "Maybe. But let me tell you, all governments and all banks daily totter on the brink because of men and women who can break their codes."

"Computers," Micah said. "You're going to hook Lynch up to a computer?"

"Not *hook up.* But use him to program them, yes. Or better yet, he'll give us the formulas to program them correctly. What they call in the business a *new paradigm.*"

"Unbelievable," Micah Lanscomb said. He leaned back in his chair, making it creak. His long legs flopped out in front of him as if he were somehow disconnected from them.

"And Lynch can do this?" Cueball asked.

"Yes. From my review of the file—and let me tell you, I'm no slouch at higher math, myself—this guy—"

"Murderer," Micah said. "Killer."

"Alright," Robeling continued. "This murderer, this killer, can do exactly that. One day, he may save us all."

"But not by choice," Cueball said.

"But not by choice," Robeling repeated.

Two minutes ticked by while the three men sat there. The light outside grew brighter.

"I'm hungry," Cueball said.

"Huh?" Micah asked.

"I said I'm hungry. Let's go get a bite to eat."

"Just one damned minute, Cueball. First, Special Agent Shane By-God Robeling, where are you taking Lynch?"

"There's this old manor house right outside of Arlington, Virginia—"

[43]

Cueball and Micah were waiting at Nell's when Leland Morgan arrived.

"Does anybody know what really happened this morning?" Morgan asked as he took a seat at their table. "I mean why in the hell the feds—"

"Shut up," Cueball told him. "The way I see it, Morgan, you've got a hell of a lot of explaining to do."

Morgan frowned. "Look. I don't have to explain myself to the likes of you, Boland. But I'll tell you only so you don't blame me for something that was clearly your own damned fault. Twenty minutes before you got there, Robeling showed up with two carloads of suits flashing FBI badges. They collected all of our police radios and car keys and made us all wait in a parking lot five blocks away until it was all over. They wanted Lynch and I didn't have the authority to stop them."

Cueball studied the man for a long moment, his gaze unblinking. "According to Robeling, you were supposed to have called us off, let us know they had Lynch in custody."

The corners of Morgan's mouth turned upward, however slightly. It was apparent he was trying hard to suppress a grin.

"I get it," Micah said to Morgan. "You wanted either one or both of two outcomes. You either wanted me to kill Lynch, or you wanted Robeling and his men to shoot *us*."

Morgan paused a moment. He turned his cold eyes to Micah. "Maybe the battery on my phone went dead at the wrong moment. Did you ever think of that?"

Cueball held up a hand before Micah could retort. "Then one of Robeling's men, whoever was detaining you, would have made the call himself. No. You told them you had called us off. You lied for your own reasons."

Morgan sipped at his cup of coffee. "Shit happens," he said.

Cueball chuckled. "You never did have much use for me, Morgan."

"I've told you as much already."

"Well, I suppose what's done is done," Cueball said. "It's all ancient history now. The only problem I'll have from now on is sharing this island with you. But fortunately I won't have to. Because one of us will be leaving."

"You'd better start packing, then," Morgan stated.

"Naw," Micah said. "He ain't going nowhere. And neither am I."

"Suit yourself," Morgan said. "Besides, I had nothing to do with the feds coming in here. You can blame me for not letting you know they were here, if you'd like."

Morgan began to make the motions of getting up from the table, but Micah Lanscomb reached out with the speed of a striking snake and pinned Morgan's wrist to the table.

"You want to tell him, C.C., or should I?" Micah asked.

"Tell me what?"

"Look to your right, Morgan," Cueball said. Morgan's head turned slowly to gaze out of Nell's plate glass window. Three highway patrol vehicles were there, blocking the parking lot.

"What's happening?" Morgan stated.

"The Texas Rangers are going to have a little party, Morgan. And you're the guest of honor."

"More of your political connections?" Morgan bluffed.

"It took a little bit of doing, but between Micah and myself, we did a little checking."

"It begins with the ticket," Micah chimed in. "The one you left on my security truck. You even decided to spell your name out carefully. Now while I realize it was just you being the prick you are, that's where it started. I had forgotten all about it until I realized the time was running out to either pay the damned ticket, or try to fight it in the municipal court. I normally pay my own tickets when I'm off the clock—"

"But since he technically wasn't," Cueball said, "he brought it to me. I questioned him on it. It seems you gave him the ticket on the morning of the day before Homer was killed. The morning Micah met *with* Homer."

"That means nothing," Morgan said. "Cops give out tickets."

"Not you," Cueball stated. "I did some checking at the police station in the middle of the night last night. You're too full of yourself to do menial work, except when it means, like Micah said, you *can* exercise your prerogative and be a real prick. So that was your first mistake."

"I don't follow."

"Of course you don't," Micah said. "You saw Homer talking with me. Homer knew a great deal about how things were back in the back yonder. Say, 1943."

"I don't know anything about 1943, except what you two bozos have told me," Morgan said.

"Doesn't matter," Micah said. "You saw us."

"Second," Cueball said, "you may have put one over on Mike Stratham, the desk cop at the morgue, when you went to fish the bullet out of Homer Underwood's head. All that business about not signing in and promising to bring him a cup of coffee."

"His word against mine," Morgan said. "You've got the wrong asshole, asshole."

"No," Micah said. "We've got the right asshole all right."

"The security tape, Morgan," Cueball said. "You got the autopsy doctor away from his appointed duties through a fake emergency, but you forgot that there are security tapes."

"I had to take pictures," Morgan said.

"Pictures which never happened," Micah said. "You killed my friend. The only reason I can't kill you right this minute is because there are a few Texas Rangers right outside. They're going to put you away, Morgan."

"I suspect so," Cueball said. "For a very long time."

The change came over Leland Morgan slowly. He turned and looked out Nell's plate glass window to see three men standing near their highway patrol vehicles. They were talking. One of them noticed they were being watched and shortly all three were staring back at Leland Morgan through the glass.

"Remember that rector I talked to after Homer's funeral?" Cueball asked.

"What about him?"

"If he were here right now, he would tell you that confession is good for the soul."

Morgan bent forward and spoke downward to the tabletop.

"I had to do it." he said.

Cueball and Micah waited for more.

"I was going to be a cop. One of the good guys. But there was no way up for me. I wasn't going to be a traffic cop forever. And then *she* came along. First she did some small favors for me. Then she loaned me money. Before long...she had control of my life."

"Who?" Micah asked.

"Boland will tell you," he replied.

• • •

After the Texas Rangers had taken Morgan away, Micah looked over at Cueball, who sat regarding the leavings of his breakfast.

"What?" Cueball asked.

"Do you think there's going to any big trouble about all this? You know, Old Island crap?"

"Not any trouble that I can't handle," Cueball replied. "Finish your breakfast."

• Galveston, Texas
DECEMBER 24, 1943

[44]

The front door to Hanny's place lost its hinges one after the other under the deafening blast of a shotgun. Splinters of wood and plaster flew across the slick dance floor. The doorway was hefted aside by a pair of meaty, oversized hands and disappeared into the night beyond.

Bonaparte Foley entered the room as he snapped his double-barreled shotgun closed again.

"Muldoon!" he called.

Denny Muldoon raised his pistol and aimed it at Foley.

"Here," he said.

Foley raised the shotgun and leveled it from his waist at Muldoon. He walked forward slowly, sort of an easy saunter. Foley made it appear as if it were the most natural thing in the world to walk toward a pistol pointed at him. At three paces distance he stopped.

A moment of intense quiet ensued.

"This is interesting," Longnight stated. "One never knows what will happen next."

"Is that him?" Foley asked Muldoon. "Is that Longnight?"

"Yeah."

"I'm taking him."

"Nope," Muldoon said. "He's going back to Washington. He has an appointment with some top government men. He'll help us win the war."

"With what? His knife? Or his pecker?"

"His brain," Muldoon said.

"Why don't we just cut it out and send it parcel post, then? Along with his pecker."

"What are they talking about?" Underwood asked.

"You don't want to know," Longnight stated. Longnight's eyes moved back and forth between the two lawmen. He was gauging them. Judging. After a moment, he visibly relaxed.

"Ahem," Longnight said, as if clearing his throat.

"What?" Foley asked.

"Oppenheimer has it all wrong. His equations. If you want to make a bomb with fissionable material, you have to account for the strength of the valence bands of the materials, which is actually a variable unless you can suspend it in an electromagnetic field. Then it's all equal."

"Huh?" Foley asked.

"See?" Muldoon stated.

"Two million kids," Homer Underwood said. "Wasn't that what you told me, Denny? At least two million more kids are going to die in this war in Europe and in the Pacific. Conservatively. I think that's what you said, right?"

"Yeah. That's what I said."

"One wonders," Longnight said, "how many of those boys will be from Texas."

"You've got one minute to tell me what the hell you're talking about, Muldoon. And if I'm not convinced, well, I don't care if you shoot me or not. This shotgun will blow you in half."

"Tell him," Muldoon snapped to Longnight.

Longnight enterlaced his fingers behind his head and propped his shoes up on the table in front of him.

"It's like this. They want a bomb. A bomb that can destroy an entire city with one blast. A city, say, the size of Houston."

"That's a pipe-dream," Foley said. "Science fiction."

Longnight shook his head. "I like living and breathing, and the chance to get out and about once in a while. I may have gone a little too far this time. But, this thing we're talking about. This bomb. I know how to make it."

It soon became clear in the silence that followed that Bonaparte Foley believed the dapper man sitting at the table in the colored honky tonk.

The shotgun in his hands lowered to the floor by degrees.

Galveston, Texas

OCTOBER 1987

[45]

The same day Leland Morgan was taken into custody by the Texas Rangers, Vivian DeMour stopped by the Boland home on Ball Street. She carried a brown paper sack with a twine handle. Myrna, who had returned from Tyler just after lunch, greeted Vivian like a long-lost friend.

After the obligatory hugs and chitchat were dispensed with, Myrna allowed Cueball to take Vivian's elbow and guide her out to the front porch. He set her down on Myrna's wicker settee and took a seat on the porch swing close by. He noticed the bag she was carrying with her, thought of asking what it was, but let it go. She placed it carefully on the porch beside the settee.

"I know it was hard for you to see them put Harrison in handcuffs," Cueball said.

"I don't care to discuss it, C.C.," she said.

"I realize that. But there is something I have to show you." Cueball reached into his shirt pocket and unfolded the piece of paper he had retrieved from the hall bureau while Myrna and Vivian had chatted.

"What is it?" Vivian asked.

"You'll have to see for yourself."

Vivian took the piece of paper and unfolded it slowly.

She began reading aloud.

"Lyle. Deliver the infant to the care of the rector of St. Mary's Catholic Church in Houston. You may keep one thousand of the fifty for your satisfactory performance and deliver the remainder to the rector with my admonition that it is to be…" Vivian DeMour's voice broke. Her body stiffened.

"Finish it, Vivian. Please."

"It is to be used for the child's… education. Signed, Abe."

Cueball watched as the note slowly came down to her lap. She looked up at him, her eyes brimmed with tears. And yet there was a chilling look there.

"I'm sorry, Vivian," Cueball said. "You know that partner of mine, Micah? He's a good deal more intelligent that anybody gives him credit for. He was Jack Pense's friend. After we buried Jack, Jenny gave this letter to Micah. Just yesterday, Micah gave it to me."

"My own father," Vivian said between clenched teeth. "If he wasn't dead I would kill him myself."

Cueball waited for a moment and then turned as if to go back in the house. Having decided something, he looked at her once more.

Vivian DeMour pushed at her eyes with her hands, sat a while and then looked up at Cueball. "I have something for you, Charles."

She reached down beside her and into the brown paper sack. She withdrew a brown leather book and held it out toward Cueball.

"What is it?" he asked.

"It's from Longnight. It's...I think it's important."

Cueball took the book, riffled the pages carefully.

"What should I do with it?" he asked.

"I don't know," she said.

"I can't make heads or tails of it."

"You'll know what to do," she said.

Cueball sighed. "Vivian, I wish you would have told me from the start what was in that safe that Jack Pense died to protect."

"Why?"

"I kept my end of the bargain," Cueball said, his voice soft and quiet. "I didn't let Harrison get killed like you asked. Micah would have killed him himself, but I made sure all the cartridges he loaded our guns with were dummies."

"I thank you, Charles."

There was a long silence.

"Vivian, this whole thing has bothered me from the beginning, from the moment Jack was killed and Harrison's fingerprint showed up on the warehouse safe."

Vivian remained silent, waiting.

Cueball continued, "I think he was looking for his birth certificate. He wanted to know who his father was...and his mother. But there were too many links in the chain. There was Homer Underwood and what he might have known about Harrison's birth from back when Longnight was running around scot-free on the island. But I don't think it was Harrison who killed Homer Underwood. Homer might have known about Harrison's birth, but Harrison worked with a knife. So Homer had to be gotten out of the way. The problem is, there are so damned few DeMours left. Actually, there's only the *one*. That's you."

Vivian DeMour sat rigid. If she were glass, the slightest nudge would have shattered her.

"The last heir of one of the island's wealthy families doesn't have to pull the trigger herself to get someone out of the way—someone who knew too much from long ago about who Longnight really was, and not just a name. She would simply buy someone off to do it for her. Someone, maybe, she bought off a long time ago when she had him made lieutenant of the Galveston Police Department."

"I don't know what to say, C.C."

"You don't have to say anything. The Texas Rangers will be over to your house in a while to talk with you about it. I suggest you cooperate with them. Leland Morgan is already in custody. One would wonder what he's saying to them about now."

Cueball turned to go. He almost said what was on his mind, but thought better of it. He almost said, "I should have let Micah kill him." Instead, all he could say was, "You always said that Lindy was the wild one. Now, I'm not so sure about that. Goodbye, Vivian."

· *Galveston, Texas*

SEPTEMBER 1944

[46]

Lyle's truck gave out on Bart, Lorraine and the kids—and the DeMour baby—half a mile from the Galveston ferry. The radiator had sprung a leak and the engine had overheated. Despite attempts to keep it cool with multiple stops for water along the way, the truck would go no further. They abandoned it, left the keys in the ignition and began walking.

A hundred yards up the road Bart remembered the bag behind the seat.

"Forgot something," he told Lorraine. "Be right back." Bart ran back to the truck and took the bag of money from behind the seat. He stuffed it into his duffel bag while his family stood looking back at him.

"Forgot my chewing tobacco," he said when he returned.

The ferry ride was uneventful. The kids climbed up to the upper deck and rang the bell while Bart and Lorraine, who held the baby, stood watching the tide roll across Galveston Bay. The wind was up and it whipped at them. Lorraine never once spoke, and Bart was fine with that.

They walked from the ferry landing on the Island to a service station, where Lorraine called her father to come get them. Twenty minutes later a large, black 1940 Packard Clipper rolled up. The family piled in.

The driver, Nicolas Pense, sat in stoic silence behind the wheel.

"Thank you, Daddy," Lorraine said as the family packed into the car.

Pense grunted a reply as they moved off into the evening.

• • •

Bart Dumas could never stomach the Penses—aside from Lorraine—and the feeling on their part was apparently mutual. After unloading their suitcases and Bart's duffel bag into the spare bedroom, the family wandered to the dining room for supper.

Nicholas Pense was in his late fifties. He was a soft-looking man with a permanent scowl etched into his features. He spoke little, and when he did it was to remonstrate, to carp or belittle. He had perfected this skill so that he could, with one or two words, cut to the bone, twist the blade and make you feel it. Bart hated the man beyond all forbearance, but being Bart Dumas, the wheels turned slowly, if at all, and a biting *riposte* to any comment from the old man might come hours, days, or possibly weeks later, if ever. Pense had thinning hair, wore clothes that were all the rage in upper-crust society from ten years gone, pinched every silver dollar until the eagle it bore screamed for mercy, and haunted the rooms of his spacious Sherman Boulevard home in search of something nameless. Also, he had a gun collection that rivaled a South-African Dutch campaigner. Pense's *frau* was the thoroughly repressed housewife, apathetic, servile and apt to cringe. Bart wasn't sure but that even Lorraine was embarrassed by her will-less existence.

After a near stone-silent dinner of meatloaf, over-cooked vegetable on sparkling china and stale tea in Scottish crystal—a dinner where even the children were daunted into silence by the oppressive atmosphere—Pense excused himself with a grunt and went upstairs. Shortly thereafter Lorraine excused herself as well and went in search of her old man.

• • •

Lorraine Pense Dumas entered her father's bedroom.

"Daddy?"

"Here, Princess." Pense emerged from a walk-in closet.

"Bart brought a big sack with him. It's full of money. The baby is the DeMour baby."

"I knew it the moment I picked you two up. I will not allow this family to fall through scandal. We're keeping the child. You will raise him as if he is one of your own and you will stay here with me."

"Yes, Daddy."

"The child will be given no special treatment. He is a foundling, and he'll be brought up as a foundling."

"Yes, Daddy."

"Your husband...you are done with him?"

"I'm done," Lorraine said without hesitation.

"Good. He is about to disappear from all our lives forever. You may go and cry into your pillow, if you feel the need."

"No," she said. "I am done with crying."

"That's my girl," Pense said.

• • •

Bart was sitting on the back porch regarding a seagull on top of a telephone pole along the street when Nicholas Pense stepped from the house.

"Bart," he said. "Let's go hunting." Pense handed Bart a British .303 Enfield, checked that there were no rounds in his own double-barreled shotgun and didn't wait for Bart to reply but instead started down the back steps toward the garage.

"Wait. What are we hunting?" Bart called after him and picked himself up to trail the man.

"Snipe," Pense said.

• • •

Bartholomew Dumas didn't like the Island. He never had. And life had not been going well since his last trip to the cursed place. So it was with a sense of dread that he rode beside Lorraine's father on this evening hunting trip. They had no lanterns, no flashlight that he was aware of, no gunny sacks for what they were to kill and bring back. No sir. Nothing.

Pense whistled discordantly and Bart attempted without any success to recognize the tune. After a while the old man stopped and Bart turned to watch the sun go down inland. They were heading south and away from town.

• • •

Galveston is a narrow strip of land some twenty-nine miles in length and two and a half miles in width at its widest point. The island tapers as you travel southwest until there is nothing left but the waters of San Luis Pass, a dangerous place where the rip-tide has been known to walk up and grab anyone impertinent enough to immerse themselves any further than waist-deep.

Pense pulled off the narrow, double-rutted roadway just before it played out into the water, parked on the sand and killed the engine.

"So there's snipe around here?" Bart asked.

Pense didn't say a word.

"Never killed a snipe," Bart said. "Never even seen one."

"We'll flush them out and bring home dinner for the next week." Pense smiled.

"Is it snipe season, do you think?" he asked, but the old man ignored him and climbed out into the gathering dark.

"Can't even see to shoot, really," Bart said to himself, and got out of the car. His head had begun aching ever since he'd stopped drinking. But Bart Dumas was used to living with his hangovers. His whole life had become one long, continuous hangover, and he knew nothing better to do than to keep breathing his way through it.

At that moment Pense held out a flask to him. Bart took it, unstoppered it, and sniffed.

"What's this?" he asked.

"Drink," Pense said. "It's cognac. Although I'm sure you've never tasted the stuff. It's better than beer or whiskey. It's the smart man's drink."

"Reckon I need me some of that," Bart said, and took a long pull. It went down smooth as silk.

He handed the flask back to Pense who took a long pull on it himself.

There seemed to be somebody walking close by, just out of vision, but when Bart swept his eyes that way, he could see no one. Then the fire began in his belly and all thoughts of interlopers afield left him. Bart Dumas wasn't the kind of man to let more than one thought at a time crowd him.

"Let's go down the beach a bit," Pense said. "We'll find them in the sea grass and the dunes."

"Sure thing," Bart said.

They had walked a hundred yards when he thought he heard someone call his name, as if they were over the next hill or something.

"Did you hear that?" Bart asked.

Pense shook his head.

"Alright then," Bart said. "You know, I didn't take you for the outdoors type, Nicholas. But going hunting wasn't a bad idea."

Pense nodded but kept his eyes straight ahead.

After five more minutes, with the sun gone completely from the sky and only a dim glow remained on the horizon, Pense stopped and nodded toward the dunes west of them. "You go on up there to the top of those dunes and tell me what you see. Then go along the dunes around behind them and flush them in my direction."

There it was again. A distant voice, and a voice he recognized.

"We'd better trade guns as well," Pense said. "You'll be closer to them, so you'll need the shotgun."

Bart traded with him. Pense dug in his pocket and handed Bart a couple of shells.

"Should I load up now?" Bart asked.

"Not yet. You won't need them until you see something."

"Right," Bart said.

He walked away from Pense and made his way up the lowest sand dune in sight. He wondered, absently, how anything could live amid all the sand. Crabs he could understand. Crabs were practically composed of sand, what with their shells like hard stone.

He heard the voice again, this time close. He recognized it. It was Lyle Fisher.

"That you, Lyle?" he called out. The dark was kind of funny in that it seemed to soak up all sound around him.

He stopped atop the dune.

"Lyle?" He called ahead.

And then distinctly, Lyle said: "Stupid-dead is what you are, Bart."

The hole opened in Bart's gut and a wad of his innards came tumbling out. An instant later he heard the report. He dropped the shotgun.

He turned around and gazed down the dune toward Pense.

The second bullet went through his right lung and out his back into the high sea grass.

Bart Dumas tumbled forward and rolled.

He waited to die.

Pense rolled him over, stared down into his face. Pense's face was black, and behind Pense's head the moon shone, illuminating the man's head like a nimbus crown, as if Lorraine's father was one of those saints who walked with Jesus in the Holy Land.

"Stupid dead is what you are, Dumas," Pense said. "There's no snipe. I found the money in your duffel bag. How stupid can you get? We're keeping the DeMour baby. And the money. And we'll make sure the DeMours keep paying. Nobody wants a bastard, that much is sure. The DeMours don't want him and we don't either, but we're willing to keep him for the money. Lorraine was right to tell me. You would have screwed everything up, Bart Dumas. You were stupid before. And now you're stupid-dead."

And then Pense's face became that of Lyle Fisher's.

"It hurts, Lyle. I have to...confess something," Bart said. His breath came in little hitches. He wasn't long for the world.

"What?" Lyle asked.

"Owe you a hundred...dollars," Bart said. "That's all...I took. Hundred...dollars."

And then Lyle was gone and the moon was gone and coldness tugged at him. It crept from the balls of his feet and up his calves and over his private parts and on into his head.

• Galveston, Texas

OCTOBER 1987

[47]

Two evenings later Micah and Cueball found themselves once more on the front porch. The weather was once again warm over the Gulf Coast after a few days of cool north wind. Since Myrna had returned both men knew their unsupervised evenings would be drawing to a close and the whiskey would once more come only in measured drams. But not this night. Tonight it was a liter of Glenmorangie, and the level in the bottle fell steadily and Myrna had not once interrupted them.

They talked of this and that, skirting uneasily around the edge of the recent events until at last Micah said, "C.C., I'm sorry about your friend, Vivian DeMour."

"So am I."

"It just seems like such a waste. All that fortune, all that history. For what?"

"Yeah. I spoke with the Ranger in charge of the investigation today. Vivian confessed to paying Leland Morgan to get rid of old Homer."

"Damn."

"You remember what Sheer said that Lynch told him before they let him out?"

Micah sighed. "Something about someone would have a long fall from heaven."

"I've been thinking about that. What do you think Lynch meant by that?"

Micah paused for a moment, considering. Then he said, "I think Lynch planned to kill them all. Even Vivian, who took great pains to make sure he survived. Hmph. The angel sent of God."

"Some angel," Cueball said. "More like a demon sent from hell."

"I do wonder, though," Micah said, "where Lynch was staying all that time he was on the Island."

"At a motel on the mainland. His motel room key was in his pocket. I got that information from Robeling."

"Do you really think he was trying to kill Vivian DeMour?"

Cueball paused, considering his words. He had a faraway look in his eyes. "I don't know. I think if he wanted to, he would have early on. He was a force of nature, like his father."

"I'm surprised Vivian didn't have him killed herself."

"No," Cueball said. "That's one thing she told me was not to happen. Harrison was the last of her family. And blood is always thicker than water."

The two sat for several minutes without speaking. Cueball waited for more from Micah, and he was not disappointed.

"Homer," Micah said. "And Denny Muldoon."

"Hmph."

"There was definitely something between those two."

"I suspect you're right. But then there are some things it's maybe better not knowing."

Micah sighed. "You're probably right. By the way, I know what was in the safe in the DeMour warehouse."

"So do I," Cueball said.

"Well, I shouldn't be surprised. I'm sure the feds have it all now."

"I called that Shane Robeling fellow and confirmed it," Cueball said. "Harrison Lynch's handwritten mathematical texts are now the property of the United States Government. But now I have a puzzle for *you*."

"Yeah? What's that?"

"This," Cueball said, and reached into the paper sack on the floor beside him and brought out the leather notebook Vivian had given to him, and handed it to Micah. "It's Longnight's journal, or it's a madman's ramble, or it's the future of the human race, take your pick. Regardless, it is *not* the property of the United States Government."

It was a leather journal of some age, hand-bound. Micah's hand fluttered through the pages, pausing for mere moments, then flipping forward again. His eyes moved and darted from leaf to leaf.

He began reading aloud: "'The summation: As field strength approaches infinity, gravity goes to zero.' 'In this manner instantaneous communication can be achieved between any two points anywhere in the universe.' 'Gravity is, therefore, instant, and therefore not a waveform, as one must have time against which to measure the troughs and crests of a wave.'"

Micah looked up at Cueball. The look was priceless.

"I wonder if Lynch's writing was anything like this?" Micah asked.

"I have no idea. But it must have been interesting enough for the government to want it all. No telling what madman's technology is in use today because of the father. Or what might be in the future from the son."

"By the way, Homer once told me I should find out who Lynch really was, and by that he meant who Lynch's father really was. Do you know who Longnight was?"

Cueball took a sip of his whiskey and turned slowly to Micah. "Longnight? I don't know who he was. I rather imagine he was a nobody. But he was apparently brilliant when it came to the things you're reading there in that journal of his. I think he was a surgeon of some kind. Probably well-educated. Hell, for all I know he could have been royalty."

"Good God. You know, some folks think that Jack the Ripper was a member of the Royal Family. Oh cripes!"

"What?"

"His birth certificate. He was born here on the Island. There would be a record."

"Exactly," Cueball said. "There was. But when he was kidnapped and raised by the Penses, they didn't have a birth certificate for him. The Penses moved to Houston shortly after Harrison came to them. He was supposed to have gone to a Catholic orphanage in Houston, but somehow the kidnapping went south. Somewhere along the line Harrison found out who his real father was and what his real father's name was. And I think I know who told him who his father was. He changed his last name to Lynch right before his first killing spree."

Micah thought on it. "Homer," he said.

"That's what I figure," Cueball agreed.

"Where *is* the birth certificate?"

"The last of the DeMours has it."

"Vivian," Micah said. "That's what Lynch was really after when he robbed the warehouse and killed his stepbrother."

"Yeah. He wanted his identity," Cueball agreed. "He wanted to know who both his mother and his father really were, and not what he may have been told by the Penses or anyone else. The official birth record was taken from the county shortly after Lynch's birth. A little petty bribery, I suspect. I'd lay odds on it having been Abraham DeMour."

A light breeze sprang up to rustle the palm fronds in the trees beside the house, and the faint whisper of the surf could be heard as the Gulf rolled endlessly onto the beach. Micah smiled and sipped his scotch and said no more.

As for his part, Cueball could have said some things as well. He could have said that he had noted Denny Muldoon's former caregiver Minnie stepping inside Micah's trailer late last night when he had come by for a visit, but had instantly decided not to intrude on the couple. Diana, gone these many years, no doubt would have approved. Cueball had never known Micah's Diana, but if she was half the gentle and caring creature Micah had described to him, then she should be smiling.

Cueball could have also mentioned that he had lied when he told Micah and Morgan that Lindy DeMour was Harrison Lynch's mother. He could have gone on to explain that he did so because Lindy, now dead these many years, was beyond any harm or shame, while his friend Vivian was still very much alive. She would stand trial for Homer Underwood's murder. There was still the one secret—the identity of the father and the love of the mother for her son despite the murderous natures of all three—father, son *and* mother. Justice, though. Justice, perhaps, would not be too unkind to Vivian DeMour.

"Old Island shit," Micah would have called it—all of it—his voice tinged with mild disapproval. Cueball decided to remain silent on the subject as the two of them sat cloaked in the soft sounds of the late fall night, each lost in his own thoughts as they gazed out into the balmy darkness that lay over the town like a shroud.

Finis

AN AUTHOR'S NOTE

Milton T. Burton passed away in the early morning hours of December 1, 2011. He will be missed by his family, his friends—many of whom were of the life-long variety—and by his many fans.

I want to say a few words, both about the current volume and about my friend.

Galveston is the central character in this story. As Milton says, "There has always been something a little sad about Galveston." I agree with him. I love Galveston, having spent many summers there in my youth. But to go there again, to re-create it as it once was in all its splendor and all its tarnish. That is a dream. And now it's a dream come true.

Along about the summer of 2011, Milton went into the hospital. His health deteriorated rapidly.

At the time of Milton's hospital stay he had three books out in hardback from Minotaur/Thomas Dunne Books, including *The Rogues' Game*, *The Sweet and the Dead*, and *Nights of the Red Moon*, with a fourth, *The Devil's Odds* at that time forthcoming in February of 2012. Additionally there remains his completed manuscript for *These Mortal Remains*, which I have completed editing. It is slated for publication in July 2013.

During the latter part of the summer of 2011, when *Long Fall From Heaven* was nearing completion, Milton described his ideas for the first chapter to me in detail. I had thought the first chapter we had initially written together was *the* first chapter. It wasn't. There was the other one—the one that existed only in Milton's mind. It was that chapter that my friend most wanted to write. So the file for the present volume sat for some time on my computer with the words "To Be Finished By Milton" in brackets under the first chapter heading. Then, over the summer and fall of 2011, Milton's health complications became much more complicated. On my last visit to him in late November, mere days before his death, I knew the end was likely near. I hurried back home to Austin from Tyler and polished up the present volume the best I could. As I sat thinking about my friend before my computer and the unfinished text of this volume, I remembered his descriptive words to me for the first chapter. I remembered the *feel* of the words as he described Longnight's stay at the government's mental asylum. With Milton's words set clearly in my mind, I began.

I believe I have captured that feel here.

I would like to thank Milton's family—his sons Seth, David and Thomas, and his daughter Samantha—for permitting the publication of this work. Thanks are also due to David Hudson, of Tyler, Texas, perhaps Milton's oldest and best friend, for approving this book for publication as the executor of Milton's estate.

Additionally, my thanks go out to Bobby Byrd, Lee Merrill Byrd, and Johnny Byrd of Cinco Puntos Press for this lovely edition. You folks are the greatest.

There are many people—far too many to name—who helped this author along the way. You know who you are, and I believe you know the depth of my gratitude.

My final thanks are to Milton T. Burton, for understanding and sage advice when it was most needed, for late night phone calls, Mexican food and fine cigars, and for being who he was—writer, educator, historian, mentor, and above all, friend. I miss you.

This book has been a labor of love and tender care. The subject matter is dark, needless to say, but darkness is the true nature of both crime and crime fiction. It is my sincere hope that this book is true to Milton, to Galveston—both as it is and as it was—and true to Texas and to history. I believe that Milton and I have accomplished all of these, and more.

George Wier
Austin, Texas
February 2013